What Is This Thing Called Love?

GENE WILDER

What Is This Thing Called Love?

ST. MARTIN'S PRESS
New York

This is a work of fiction. All of the characters, organizations, and events portrayed in this novel are either products of the author's imagination or are used fictitiously.

www.stmartins.com

Library of Congress Cataloging-in-Publication Data

Wilder, Gene, 1935–
    What is this thing called love? / Gene Wilder.—1st ed.
        p. cm.
    ISBN 978-0-312-59890-7
    1. Love stories, American.   I. Title.
    PS3623.I5384W47 2010
    813'.6—dc22

                                            2009040236

First Edition: March 2010

10 9 8 7 6 5 4 3 2 1

To my cousin, Buddy Silberman, who inspired three of these stories. When he was alive he really wanted love, but settled only for sex.

Contents

Prelude

Apart from the 1929 Cole Porter song, this is a ridiculous title and I know it; sounds a little like some egotistical guru telling the rest of the world about love and lovemaking and broken hearts—as if most people didn't already know these things from their own experiences. And yet . . . some of the desperately romantic situations I've known, plus a few touching and sometimes comical situations I've heard from others, might give you a little pleasure and a laugh. If they do, I'll be happy.

—GENE WILDER

What Is This Thing Called Love?

The Birthday

Rumor has it that Buddy Silberman drove up to Caesars Palace one afternoon with his best friend, Sonny Hurwitz, and was seen at the craps tables that evening, where Buddy was overheard making a bet with Sonny that he was either going to make forty thousand "smackers" that night or walk out of the hotel naked.

It was cold and raining at four in the morning when Buddy walked out of Caesars Palace, stark naked except for the *L.A. Times* wrapped around his waist.

As he hurried into Sonny's car, the night doorman heard Sonny call out, "You jerk—I wouldn't have held you to your bet."

Buddy answered, "A bet is a bet—I'm not a welcher—now get me the hell out of here."

Sonny and Buddy lived and worked in Los Angeles selling wireless cable television. While they were having lunch at Junior's delicatessen, their usual eatery, Sonny decided to take the bull by the horns.

"I wanna ask you something seriously, Buddy."

"Shoot," Buddy said.

"Have you ever been in love?"

"Of course! All the time," Buddy answered. "I'd go crazy if I wasn't in love once in a while."

"You really mean it?"

"Sure. When we were growing up, did you ever see a train standing in Milwaukee station, waiting to get started?"

"Yeah . . ." Sonny answered, not having a clue where Buddy's mind was headed.

"Then all of a sudden you hear a big blast and the engine shoots out this gigantic gust of steam, maybe twenty, thirty feet in the air, like an explosion?"

"So?"

"That's what I'm talking about, Sonny."

"What the hell have choo-choo trains got to do with being in love?" Sonny asked, almost choking on his corned beef sandwich.

"YOU'VE GOT TO GET RID OF THE POISONS, SONNY! You can't let them sit inside your nuts and wait for them to explode. You gotta release all that stuff or you'll go nuts. Didn't you ever study mental health in high school?"

Sonny took a long pause before answering. Buddy's weird metaphors always drove him crazy.

"You're talking about sex, Buddy. I'm talking about love."

"Same difference."

"Buddy . . . when you invite a young lady to your boudoir, how much time do you actually spend with her?"

"Into my WHAT?"

"Your bedroom! Didn't you learn any French when you were taking all those mental health classes?"

"Sure! Voo lay voo voo coo shay avec moi? They understand that."

"Who understands that?" Sonny asked, getting more and more annoyed.

"French broads."

"Why do you insult women by calling them broads?" Sonny asked.

"Because Sinatra does," Buddy answered.

Sonny took a deep breath and exhaled slowly. "And supposing she's not French?"

"I say it anyway—makes a good impression. You wanna go to Mateo's for dinner tonight?"

"Not tonight, Buddy. I've got a date with a very nice *woman*. I'll see you tomorrow."

Buddy went to dinner alone at Mateo's, where there was a movie star eating in the booth next to him almost every time he went. When he got home he found a note under his door.

> Buddy. I'm free tonight. If you want me to come over, call me.
>
> xoxo Carol What's Her Name

Buddy had to look up her telephone number under W, for "What's Her Name," because he had a terrible memory when it came to last names.

Carol What's Her Name came to Buddy's apartment at 10:30 p.m., as Buddy had requested. When she came in they greeted each other like old pals.

"How ya doin'?" she asked, as she gave him a nice little hug and took off her jacket.

"Doing good," Buddy answered. "You want something to drink?"

"Sure! What have you got?"

"I got a half bottle of Chianti, but I opened it three days ago. It's probably still good."

"You don't have any whiskey, do you?"

"Sorry. I got whatcha callit—Crème de something—if you want?"

"No, no, that's all right." she said. "You wanna start?"

"Sure."

They went into Buddy's bedroom. The TV was on, of course . . . some movie in black and white, with Fred Mac-Murray.

Carol What's Her Name began undressing.

"You want me to undress you, Buddy? You like that sometimes."

"No, that's all right. I'm hot to trot."

Ten minutes later, just when Fred MacMurray was running away from Marjorie Maine, Buddy got out of bed, gave Carol What's Her Name fifty dollars, and said, "Thanks."

"Anytime, Buddy," she said as she put on her jacket. "And one day you're gonna remember my last name."

"What was it again?" Buddy asked.

"Berger. BERGER! Just think of hamburgers and you can't go wrong. Are you going to walk me to the door?"

"Of course."

They walked through the living room and Buddy opened the door for her. She gave him a quick kiss on the cheek and left.

Buddy went back to his bedroom to watch the end of the movie, which he had never turned off. When it was over, he took out the Sharp pocket telephone directory from his end table drawer, deleted "What's Her Name," and, under K, he wrote "Ketchup."

A week later, on Buddy's forty-eighth birthday, Sonny treated him to the Japanese restaurant that everyone was raving about, Kamegashi Sushi.

It was jam-packed, but Sonny had made a big fuss on the phone a week earlier when he'd made the reservation. He said he had to have a nice table because his friend just got out of the hospital and it was his birthday and Kamegashi Sushi was his favorite restaurant in Los Angeles. He also told the lady on the phone that Buddy was a big Hollywood producer. It worked.

An attractive Japanese woman—thin as a needle, with shiny black hair and wearing a very attractive black dress—greeted them at the door. Sonny recognized her voice from the telephone and figured that she must be the maître d'.

"Hi, I'm Sonny Hurwitz," he said to her. "I believe we

spoke to each other on the phone last week. Thanks so much for the reservation. May I present Mr. Buddy Silberman, the Hollywood producer I told you about. He just got out of the hospital yesterday."

The woman introduced herself as Kayoko. She gently took Buddy's arm and walked him past the long sushi bar. All the sushi chefs yelled "Hai!" and nodded their heads as Buddy and Sonny passed by. Kayoko led them to a semi-private table in the corner. Buddy couldn't figure out why they were getting special treatment. Sonny hadn't told him about the producer business, but Buddy wasn't complaining. He also took a fancy to this young lady, who seemed genuinely concerned about making him comfortable.

When they were seated, Kayoko said, "Would you like me to bring you lovely things to eat . . . some of our specialties . . . if you trust me?"

Buddy burst out with, "I trust ya, honey! Sorry—what's your name again?"

"Kayoko . . . Can you say?"

"Of course I can say 'Kay-O-Ko!' Hey, look at that—I can speak Japanese." Kayoko laughed.

"All right now, can you say 'Buddy'?" he asked.

"Bud-dy," she said. "Oh, look—I speak English." And they all laughed again.

"Would the gentlemen like some hot sake?" Kayoko asked.

"I don't know about the gentlemen, but *we* certainly would," Buddy answered, and cracked up over his silly joke.

Kayoko made a tiny bow and left. Buddy watched her as she walked away.

"My kinda woman," he said.

"Why's that?" Sonny asked.

"She's short. She's got a sense of humor. And she smells good."

"You should ask her to marry you."

"Maybe I will. First we gotta see how good the food is."

A waiter came to their table, holding a tray with two small jars of sake and two little cups. He placed them on the table.

"Hot sake," he said as he poured a little in their cups, then gave a polite bow and left.

"Happy birthday, kid," Sonny said as he raised his cup. "God bless you."

They clicked their sake cups and took a sip.

"Yum!" Sonny said. "This is the best sake I've ever had."

"She sure is," Buddy said as he turned to look for Kayoko.

A few minutes later, Kayoko walked in with a tray of things that smelled sensational.

"Whoa! Whatcha got there, Kayoko?" Buddy asked, as if he was about to burst into song.

Kayoko leaned over Buddy's shoulder. While she was close to his cheek, she said softly: "Buddy, I bring you and your good friend some sashimi salad and meguro tuna hand rolls with Japanese mayo and blanched asparagus . . . and a few soft-shell crab hand rolls, warm and very special."

She artistically poured each of them a little more sake in their tiny cups. "I hope you enjoy," she said, made a little bow, and left.

"Oy yoi yoi! I could get used to this, Sonny."

After their delicious appetizers, they had tiger shrimp in a special sauce and black cod in miso sauce. They were both stuffed, but Kayoko walked in carrying a tiny sponge cake with one lit candle.

"Happy birthday to you, Buddy."

Before Buddy could blow out the candle, Sonny jumped up and said, "Wait—let me take a picture! Kayoko, you get in there, too."

He had his little Minolta all ready. Kayoko leaned down and rested her cheek on Buddy's cheek.

"Say 'cheese' or 'yummy' or something," Sonny said just before he took the photo.

"One for protection," Buddy said before Kayoko could remove her cheek. He didn't care about the picture; he wanted her cheek against his for a few more seconds.

"Great! Got it," Sonny said.

Kayoko got up and took Sonny's camera.

"Now you two together and I take picture."

Sonny kneeled down next to Buddy and imitated Kayoko, rubbing his cheek against Buddy's.

"Yes," Kayoko shouted. "Good picture. Two nice friends."

On their way out of the restaurant, Kayoko walked them to the sidewalk.

"Happy birthday, Buddy-san. Good life for you, always," and she gave him a little kiss on the cheek.

"Good night, Sonny-san," she said.

Kayoko bowed and went back into the restaurant.

"You know what I like about Japanese girls?" Buddy asked as they walked to Sonny's car.

"What?"

"They don't look at how short a guy is or that I got eczema on my face."

"You think all Japanese girls do that?"

"Yeah," Buddy said with authority.

"How many have you met?"

"Two, but this one's the best."

"And what if you run out of Japanese girls?"

"Then I go to nice 'fifty dollars a throw' girls. They don't mind, either, if I'm short and have eczema."

Sonny was out of town for three weeks on business. As soon as the plane landed he called Buddy.

"I'm back! Where do you want to go for dinner tonight? WAIT! I know the answer: Kamegashi Sushi, right?"

"Nah, I'm tired of Japanese food," Buddy said.

"Don't you want to see Kayoko?"

"Nah, she's a little bit of a drag."

"What're you talking about? You wanted to marry her last week."

"I'll tell ya later. I feel like a steak tonight."

That night they went to the Palms restaurant. Buddy ordered a twenty-two-ounce porterhouse steak for two, for himself. Buddy wasn't much of a drinker, but after a shot of Absolut with his shrimp cocktail he had a glass of Merlot with his steak and fries.

"Tell me about Kayoko," Sonny said.

"I went to her restaurant a couple times while you were gone. She was sweet and nice like always, and all of a sudden she wants to get married. She scared me to death. I mean, she's a nice girl and I liked her and all . . . but, Jesus! Marriage?"

"Were you two ever—?"

"I kissed her once, on the cheek, when I was leaving the restaurant. After that she drove me crazy with the marriage business and 'Let's get married,' and 'I take good care of you.' I mean—Jesus, these Japanese girls."

A few months later, Buddy was in Las Vegas for business, not gambling. Sonny was alone one night and felt like eating Japanese food and drinking some hot sake, but he didn't want to run into Kayoko at Kamegashi Sushi, so he went to a new place he'd heard about, Kotobuki, in Venice. Not in Italy, of course, just near the ocean in L.A.

He walked in, and there to greet him was Kayoko. Talk about coincidence, he thought. She was polite and friendly, as always, and led him to a small table in the corner. She brought him some hot sake and poured a small cup for herself, too. They toasted each other with "Kampai." As she was about to leave, Sonny said, "Wait! Kayoko, forgive me—would you please tell me what happened with you and Buddy?"

"Oh, it was very sad. I'm sorry."

"Tell me about it, please. I think you broke his heart, Kayoko. But maybe he broke your heart, I don't know. I just want to find out what really happened."

Kayoko looked at the floor for several seconds. "I like Buddy. He is a nice man. But when he wanted to get married after we met only two times—"

"Wait a minute. Are you saying *he* was the one who wanted to get married?"

"I'm sorry—I couldn't marry him. I don't love Buddy. I don't even *know* Buddy. He came to Kamegashi Sushi almost every night and would say he wanted to marry me . . . first, like a little joke, but then serious. Very serious. And he would beg me to 'Just give it a try, honey.' I had to leave my job because I was so sad for him and afraid that he would keep coming to the restaurant."

Sonny was flabbergasted. He said a few nice things to Kayoko and told her it wasn't her fault at all, and that Buddy was a crazy guy. He wished her a happy life. She said, "Thank you, Sonny-san."

Sonny went to Buddy's apartment a week later. He and Buddy played poker with a few friends once a week at each other's home or apartment. It was Buddy's turn. Sonny didn't have the guts to talk to him about Kayoko, but he was sure that she had told him the truth.

In the middle of the poker game they all took a coffee and cake break. Sonny had to use the toilet, but one of the guys was in the guest bathroom, so he asked Buddy if it would be all right to use the one off his bedroom. Buddy said, "Sure!"

Buddy's TV was on, of course, and his bed wasn't made up because the maid only came in once a week.

Just before going into the bathroom, Sonny saw the photo he had taken of Kayoko and Buddy on his birthday. Kayoko was smiling as she leaned against Buddy's cheek. Buddy had put the photo into a beautiful silver frame and placed it on the night table, next to his bed. Sonny had never seen him looking so happy.

In Love for the First Time

DAVID

My name is David Marsh. I fell in love only once in my life, in Paris. Her name was Lily Sachs. In 1953 I was twenty-one years old and I went to study orchestral composition. Lily was studying piano at the Paris conservatory.

I saw her coming out of her lesson one afternoon and as she passed in front of me with some of her girlfriends, who were chattering and giggling about music and food and the French language and bidets and making love—she never noticed me. If she had given me just the hint of a smile I think I would have asked her out on the spot, but . . . oh, God . . . I wish I wasn't such a shy nincompoop.

LILY

I'm Lily Sachs. When I met David Marsh in Paris I thought he was a funny duck; tall, thin, dressed like a pauper, and always bent over, as if he were trying to hide from something. He was living in the same student residential housing where I live—the French call it a *cité*. His room was one floor above mine. I thought David was sort of obliquely handsome, and he had a sweet, gentle nature, but, oh my goodness, was he shy.

DAVID

Lily was cute more than she was beautiful, and her sensuous body sent chills through me. She had such a direct, very frank way of talking, which at first gave me the willies, but then made me envious. I finally asked Lily to go to dinner with me, dutch. I was hoping that wouldn't offend her, but I didn't have a lot of money to live on.

LILY

One evening in late September, David asked if I would like to go to dinner with him at this wonderful bistro he had heard of that specialized in Lyonnaise cooking. Before I could answer yes or no, he shouted, "dutch," meaning that we would have to split the bill. I didn't know what Lyonnaise cooking was, and even though I had only seen David two or three times in the hallways at the conservatory, he seemed like a gentleman, so I said yes.

I also thought it might be nice to go to a real French restaurant. I had been going to the brasserie around the corner for my breakfast—usually an omelet with ketchup, and a bifteck with pommes frites and plenty of ketchup for dinner—but the waiters struggled to understand me. I'm taking French lessons now—three mornings a week—so I can learn how to say "ketchup" with a French accent so they'll know what I'm talking about.

David and I met in the lobby of the *cité* that evening. He was wearing a crinkled tan sport jacket over a crinkled white shirt with a crinkled frayed collar. I wore a simple light blue dress that my mom thought looked typically French, even though she bought it at J.C. Penney.

Since it was a warm night, we walked for almost half a mile to this bistro David had heard about. I'll tell you something—he's certainly not a talker. After about ten minutes of trying to decipher his shy mumblings and getting tired of constantly asking, "What did you say, David?" we arrived at this small Lyonnais restaurant, called Chez Pauline.

What a smell when we walked in: garlic and sausages and chickens and rosemary. There were only twelve tables in the whole place, each of them covered with clean brown paper instead of tablecloths. I'm sure the purpose of that was to save money, but it also made it look like people were coming there to eat, not to admire the décor.

David ate his dinner like there was no tomorrow. My guess is that he hadn't eaten a real meal for quite some time, but I don't believe he asked me out just so I would split the bill; I think he liked me, which he showed in the most subtle ways, like holding my hand when we crossed the street on the way to the restaurant and then holding onto it a little longer than was actually necessary after we had already crossed to the other side. If I can get him to walk and talk, I think I might like him.

It was still light outside when David and I walked back to the *cité*. I can't say that I never saw Paris before, because of course I had, but I suppose I didn't really look at what was in front of me. It was remarkable how my emotions that night made a difference in the way I saw things. I suddenly noticed how crooked the shops were—I mean that buildings were designed with curves instead of all the rectangles I grew up with in New York.

I'm not shy and David is, so I decided to take the bull by the horns. As we passed a uniquely crooked bookstore, I said:

"Afraid to hold my hand, David?"

Without looking or talking, David reached down and took my hand.

"Do you live in London because your father is English?" I asked quickly, to cover any embarrassment he might be feeling.

"No, my father came from Russia. He died two years ago. It's my mother who's English. She came from London on a one-week tour of New York and met this handsome tour guide named Marshevsky . . . who changed his name later to Marsh . . . and they got married."

"How romantic."

As we crossed the avenue de l'Opéra, David put his arm around my waist and pulled me a little closer to him, "protecting me," as the crazy drivers whizzed by. I thought he was finally getting a little amorous, but when we got to the other side of the avenue he loosened his grip. He was afraid, I suppose, that I would think he was being too forward.

"How old are you, David?"

"Twenty-one."

"Me too. I think I can see your mother's rosy English cheeks in your face, and probably her straight nose . . . but I would bet that your crazy hair and eyebrows come direct from Russia."

"You'd be right."

When we walked into the lobby of our *cité*, David stood as still as a statue for almost a full minute, still holding my hand. He kept gazing up and down and around, but not at me. Then he suddenly turned and stared into my eyes, as if he were trying to decide something monumental.

"Are you a virgin?" he finally asked.

"Yes," I answered, as my heart began to pound so loudly that I could hear it.

"Me too," he said, then shook my hand politely, mumbled something like "glad . . . enjoyed . . . nice . . . you," and walked up the stairs to his room.

No kiss, I thought to myself . . . but he came damn close.

DAVID

Two nights after the night I chickened out of kissing her and almost got sick because my stupid shyness kept me from doing what I really wanted to do, Lily asked me out.

What Is This Thing Called Love?

LILY

I asked David to go to the Paris Opera House with me to see *The Elixir of Love*, by Donizetti. I don't think he had a suit because when we met in the lobby of the *cité* he was wearing that same tattered sport jacket, but he must have ironed his shirt with the frayed collar . . . and he wore a beautiful yellow tie with blue flowers printed on it. I doubted he had ever worn it before. I was wearing one of my mother's dresses—lilac and pink—which she said I should save in case I had any "romantic evenings."

We walked up about five thousand stairs to get to the cheapest seats in the theater. I wanted to see this opera because I heard it was so funny and sad, and very romantic. I invited David partly because I knew he couldn't afford it, but also because I thought the story might inspire him to be a little more aggressive.

"What's it about?" David asked as the lights began to dim.

"It's about a sweet, innocent boy named Nemorino—who is a little bit like you, David—and he worships the prettiest and richest young woman in the village. But she won't give him a tumble, even though she secretly cares for him, and he wonders how a fool like himself could possibly win her love."

"Shhh," someone behind us whispered loudly.

When the opera was over, the evening was balmy and the sky was filled with thousands of stars as David and I walked back to the *cité*. He was silent for several minutes, thinking about the music, I supposed, but when we crossed avenue de l'Opéra he finally spoke.

"If she was really so fond of him, why on earth didn't she just let him know? Why put him through such torture, making him do all those crazy things?"

"Well, for one thing, there wouldn't have been an opera."

"Sure, yes, of course. But I still think she was cruel, and probably enjoying it."

"What would you want her to do?"

"Just say, 'Nemorino, I'm very fond of you.' And that's it."

"David, I'm very fond of you and that's it."

His face turned red. He stopped walking and looked at me.

"Are you—now wait! Are we talking about the opera, or something else?"

"Something else."

"Did I do something—I mean, is there something you want me to do?" he said, turning his head away to look at a passing car.

"Keep looking at *me*, David." When he turned his head back to me I said, "What would you like to do?"

After what seemed like half an hour, he answered.

"Kiss you."

"So?"

"But we're standing on a sidewalk across from the opera house, next to all these cars whizzing by, and in the middle of all the honking and thousands of people pouring out of the opera, watching us."

"*Hundreds* of people, David—don't exaggerate! And they're not watching *us*—they're too busy talking about their own lives and desires and which restaurant they should go to for supper. And anyway . . . who cares if they do watch?"

David looked at his shoes for several seconds. "I like your dress," he said.

"Thank you."

He looked up and stared directly at me. "Your eyes are blue and gray and a little green."

"Yes, I've seen them," I said.

He leaned over, tenderly put his arms around my shoulders, and kissed me. He kept his lips on mine for at least an hour or two. I mean, for a minute or two. I wouldn't be shocked if this were the first time he'd ever kissed a young woman.

DAVID

I was just in paradise. But what would I have done if she hadn't given me a little encouragement?

LILY

David held my hand as we walked over a bridge they call the Bridge of Alexander III. There were beautiful tall lamps on each side of the bridge that looked like they were a hundred years old. We stopped halfway across the bridge and leaned over the railing to see the Seine floating underneath us, almost like quarter notes and eighth notes rushing to go home. And David was still holding my hand.

When we arrived back at the *cité* and were inside the lobby, he kissed me again.

"Good night, Lily. Thank you for a wonderful opera."

"Good night, David."

Well, it took a little work, but he kissed me. I don't know why I'm so attracted to this mumbling, tortuously shy musician, but I suppose if you always knew the "why" about such things, the meaning of life wouldn't be a mystery.

As I watched him walk up the stairs to his room, I thought, "What a cute fanny he has."

DAVID

Now what do I do? I like her so much that my body is quivering, but I can't just knock on her door at this hour and say, "Here I am! Could I have some more kissing, please?"

LILY

A little after midnight there was a knock at my door. I was still awake, thinking about the opera and the kiss that David gave me in the middle of Paris. If it had been loud knocking I would have guessed that there was a fire, but with a gentle tapping I knew it must be David.

I opened the door and there he was, standing in the hallway in plaid pajamas that had seen better days. His bright, piercingly brown eyes looked moist, as if he'd been crying. I stood in the doorway watching him in my flannel shorty. I waited several seconds for him to say something.

"Did you want to borrow a cup of sugar, David?"

"No, I . . . want to borrow you."

Now, that was the boldest sentence I'd ever heard him speak. I took his hand and led him to my bed. A little moonlight was sneaking through the only window in my small room.

If David's midnight appearance was for sex, then all of my "Miss Know-It-All" aggression was a sham. I've kissed a few men—not many, but a few—and I've hugged them on occasion and let them hug me, and in that regard I was more experienced than David. But of actual *lovemaking*, I had no experience. Still, my mother told me that there would be days (or nights) like this, and she told me what to do and how to protect myself and that I shouldn't be embarrassed or expect too much at first.

"Did you want to make love with me, David?"

"Yes."

"Why don't we lie down together for a little while . . . then, who knows what might happen?"

I sounded like a woman who had had hundreds of love affairs, but I could hear my heart pounding in my ears again. We sat on my rather smallish bed for a minute or two, just holding hands. Then, without any prompting from me, David took my face into his hands and began kissing my eyebrows and cheeks and then my lips.

"Would you like to see me naked, David?"

"Yes."

"Why don't we both take off our pajamas?"

When David saw me naked he seemed astounded.

"Not quite what you expected, David?"

"More than I expected. You're beautiful. I hope I don't disappoint you."

"As long as you keep kissing me, you have nothing to worry about."

He did keep kissing me and when he entered me—with my helping hand—it felt very nice.

David reached a climax very early; I came close, but I knew not to expect too much. He held me in his arms for ten or fifteen minutes as we both lay on the bed, looking at the moon through my window. I fell asleep with my head on his arm. We stayed that way till the sun woke us. (I had forgotten to pull the drape across my window.) David put on his pajamas, kissed me again, and walked back to his room. The next morning, I wrote to my mother.

Dear Mama,

I've been a very bad girl and you were right . . . it is sort of wonderful. David—the young musician I wrote to you about who walks bent over—became my first lover. He was considerate enough to ask me about my getting pregnant and I respected him for that. I told him about the diaphragm that Doctor Sabetta gave me.

But when we made love—which was the first time for him too—he was sweet and gentle, as always . . . but oh so tentative. It's not that I didn't enjoy it, but I was hoping that once we were actually doing it, passion would sweep over him like a rainstorm and wash away that shy, sweet, nice, kind, etc., boy. But . . . this was only our first time.

Love,
Lily

DAVID

I don't believe I sent Lily into ecstasy last night. I was too excited to realize what I was doing—even if I knew what to do. But she was always kind and I loved holding her naked body after she fell asleep on my arm. I was too damn shy, I know that, but I don't want to buy a bunch of books about how a man is supposed to thrill a woman while making love. They'd probably all be in French anyway. Lily said I didn't need books . . . that I should just play with her a little. She also told me how I might even use my tongue, which I would never have guessed in a million years.

LILY

One week later:

Dear Mama:

David and I made love two more times last week. Just to show you how much my French has improved, get a load of this:

> Mon coeur est plein de joie.

Translation: "My heart is filled with joy." You were right, Mama . . . it just takes a little time.

Love,
Lily

The Lady with the Red Hat

My name is Richard Bellsey and I'm a writer, not very famous, but I make a fairly good living. My books are mostly about love, which I understand more from longing than experience. I've only had two affairs in my life: The first was very awkward because I was painfully ignorant about lovemaking; the second affair was sublime and I was never so happy in my life. But after six months of heaven—and just before I was going to propose—the beautiful young lady ran off with a tall, handsome millionaire.

After grieving for almost a year, trying to rekindle my self-esteem, my heart began to heal and I found myself thinking of women again. Then I began dreaming about women and yearned to hold another one in my arms.

I moved from Manhattan to a little town in Vermont called Barnard. It was June 25, 2007, when I returned to my small colonial home after a long book tour. It was raining lightly that morning, but when it stopped I decided to take a walk outside and see how my little flower garden was doing. I wasn't disappointed: Spring had sprung and the roses and irises I had planted last fall were bursting with color.

As I was walking around my yard I saw a woman who was gardening in the yard next door, in back of what was popularly known as the Hunter Mansion. She was wearing an old blue jacket, muddy gardening gloves, rubber boots, a multicolored skirt that fell below her knees and flared out as she walked, and a gigantic red hat that covered her face and neck.

I had no idea if I had seen this woman before because I couldn't see her face—not underneath that red hat—but the bushes and the tall swamp maple trees that she kept ducking behind and in front of as she gardened couldn't hide her body, which was very attractive. Even the way she walked through the mud was alluring.

I had an impulse to holler out "Hi, there—I'm back home," but I suddenly got embarrassed at the possibility that she was married, or living with her significant other, or might not know who the hell I was. Of course, to be fair, I'm not sure if I had ever met her. If I had, it would have been at the Hunter Mansion's open house last Christmas, which was only a few months after I had moved in.

How strange to be so mesmerized by a clothed woman's body, accompanied by rubber boots and large dirty gloves as she gardened in the mud. Am I that frustrated? Well, if I should bump into her one of these days, and *if* she gives me a warm smile and remembers meeting me, I'll start throwing my shy charm her way and see if she responds.

On July 1, I received an invitation in the mail:

COME WATCH THE FIREWORKS WITH US AT

MR. HUNTER'S

Food! Wine! Dessert!

Friday evening, July 4th, 7:00 p.m. till midnight.

Hmm . . . I wonder who 'us' is. Well, I'll go to the party and find out.

How shall I dress? Casual or more formal, I wondered. I didn't want to get all dressed up to meet the mystery woman and then find that none of the other men at the party were wearing suits and ties. I decided to split the difference: light blue shirt under a tan sport jacket, dark blue slacks, and light brown shoes with light blue socks. Too much blue? Maybe, but I feel safer in blue.

On the evening of the party I walked to the front of the Hunter Mansion, wondering if the woman in the red hat was married to Mr. Hunter. The sun was beginning its descent behind the trees, bathing the house in a wash of fairytale gold. I had never looked at the house from the front before; it was like an English manor house, with a front door that was at least fourteen feet high. You could put my colonial into Mr. Hunter's mansion at least four times and there would still be room left over.

I assumed that Mr. Hunter must be English, filthy rich, and probably had had this house built in the late 1980s.

The picture I had in my mind was that he was tall and probably very handsome. When I thought of Mr. Hunter, I began to feel small and stupid. What on earth was I expecting—that the woman I was obsessing over would hold my hand and squeeze it while her tall, handsome husband greeted me at the door?

I rang the bell. A very polite butler let me in and told me to follow the noise to the parlor. I could hear the party going full blast. As I approached the open parlor door, a lovely woman came out. She was wearing an elegant, very flimsy, very sexy silk pants suit. Was this the woman in the muddy gloves and large red hat who had enchanted me?

"Mr. Richard Bellsey," she announced more than asked as she took my hand. "The wonderful author who lives next door."

"Well, you have the name and occupation right," I said. "I don't know about the 'wonderful.'"

"Don't be so modest, dear. We all know about you," she said as she gave me a hug and squeezed my hand. And kept holding on to it. Whether this was the woman in the red hat I couldn't tell, but her figure was beautiful. The warmth of her moist hand sent shivers through me. I'd say she was a delicious forty.

"And here comes Mr. Hunter," she said, as she led me to a small man who was walking toward us with what looked like a permanent bend in his back. He had a sweet face, a very warm smile, and was probably seventy-eight years old.

"Richard Bellsey, I want you to meet my husband, Mr. Ian Hunter. Darling, this is Mr. Bellsey, the wonderful author who lives next door."

"Lovely to see you again," Mr. Hunter said with a strong English accent and boyish enthusiasm. "Met him at our party last Christmas, wasn't it, Delia?"

"That's right, darling," she said.

"Kind of you to remember me, Mr. Hunter." *So her name is Delia.*

"Richard, come into my parlor," she said. "There are lots of hors d'oeuvres and drinks and delicious wine; just mingle and make yourself comfortable. Dinner will be at 8:30."

I mingled with the crowd. There were older couples and younger couples—probably eighteen or twenty people in all. A tall African American man was playing Cole Porter, Gershwin, and Irving Berlin on a beautifully polished Steinway piano.

I went to the mahogany table, covered with lovely white lace. It had every drink imaginable resting on it. I asked one of the barmaids if she had any white wine . . . Pinot Grigio, if possible. She reached into an ice bucket and pulled out two different brands.

"Which one would you like, sir?" she asked.

"The Livio Felluga, please."

As I wandered around the parlor, I watched the movements of the women as they danced with their husbands and lovers. It was easy to tell which was which by the way the men held their women—how closely, I mean—and the look on the women's faces. It had been so long since I had held a woman in my arms and received such a look.

After my second glass of wine I wanted to get away from all this hugging and kissing and the whispering of sweet nothings into each other's ears. I wandered through the house, not knowing exactly where I was going.

I passed through a billiard room, where two men were in the middle of a game of 8 Ball, which I knew from my army days. The gentlemen gave me a polite smile.

I walked into a huge pantry, leading into a beautiful kitchen, which had every cooking implement imaginable hanging from the ceiling. When I felt a cool breeze, I followed the smell of roses and found myself on the veranda, overlooking a pretty stream. A few smokers were out there, since there were signs all over the house saying:

NO SMOKING INSIDE THIS HOUSE!

The last reflection of sunlight was fading. Since it was close to dinnertime, I decided to go back into the house, but after walking for only a minute I must have made a wrong turn, because I realized I was lost.

I walked into an almost completely dark library. I could make out what it was because of a tiny crack in the doorway at the other end of the room, where a gleam of light shone through.

I stood still, thinking how silly it was for me to get lost. As I headed for the door, it suddenly opened, just for a second, during which I saw the silhouette of a woman. Then the door closed. Now I was in complete darkness with whoever she was.

I heard her footsteps and the rustling of clothes and then I felt a woman's arms around my neck. I heard what I was almost sure was Delia Hunter's voice, but she spoke in a gruff sort of half-whisper.

"Finally! I've been looking all over for you," she said.

I couldn't swear it was Delia, but I certainly remembered the scent of her lilac perfume when Delia came out of the parlor to greet me and held my hand. I didn't "almost taste" her perfume—I *did* taste it when she hugged me now, and I could smell it on her neck and around her ears and from under her arms.

"Delia," I whispered.

"Shhh," the voice answered. She began kissing me so passionately that I almost fell over. Then she began rubbing her body against mine and took my hand, as she kissed me, and slid it inside and down her loose silk pants and under her panties and gently directed two of my fingers into her vagina. She put my middle finger onto her clitoris as she slowly moved my finger around and up and down. I began kissing her and picturing us as we kissed. I also pictured sweet Mr. Ian Hunter, thirty-eight years older than his wife and bent over as he walked. How sexually frustrated she must be.

After a loud moan, all of her movements stopped. She gently withdrew my hand, kissed me again—just a polite kiss this time—and quickly left the room. I waited a few

seconds and then walked through the same door and found myself in the dining room.

All the guests seemed to be there, looking for their name cards. The room was illuminated by three huge chandeliers, each holding fifteen or twenty lit candles. I noticed that there were other women wearing pants suits, and some in short skirts. The parlor must have been in the next room because I heard Gershwin's "Embraceable You" coming from the piano in the parlor.

"Richard," someone hollered.

I panicked for a moment, looked up, and saw Delia waving to me to come over.

When I arrived, she said, "I want you to meet my dearest friend, Carol Gardner. Carol, this is Richard Bellsey, our resident author. You two would love each other. You're also the only singles at this whole gathering," she said with a laugh.

I shook hands with Carol Gardner and spoke some meaningless nonsense for a minute or two as I thought about my finger on Delia's clitoris only two minutes before.

After eating and drinking and chatting, I wanted to go home. I said good night to Mr. Hunter and thanked him for a wonderful party. He was as gracious as could be.

Then I found Delia. As I said good night to her, I looked straight into her eyes and saw . . . nothing! She was very polite, held my hand again as she waved good-bye to other guests, and then looked back at me.

"Good night, Richard. I hope you enjoyed our little party," she said with a smile as she hurried off.

After a restless night, remembering the touches and the kissing and the ache in my heart, I finally fell asleep.

The next morning was warm and sunny. I read my newspaper and drank some coffee, too quickly, then walked out to my yard, where I saw, bobbing up and down in the yard next door, that enormous red hat.

I was determined to see Delia again and find out—without all those people surrounding us—if last night meant anything to her. I walked slowly to where she was gardening and stood next to her. Whether she saw me or not, I don't know; she never looked up, not even once, and I still couldn't see her face underneath that ridiculously large red hat. After standing next to her for ten or fifteen seconds, I finally spoke: "Delia . . ."

The lady answered in a gruff, almost hoarse whisper. "I don't know you," she said. "And I don't talk to strangers. Whoever you are, please go away."

She moved on to the next azalea bush, but the perfume she was wearing was the same lilac scent she was wearing last night as she kissed me. It lingered in the air for several seconds after she was gone.

The Flirt

She pretended to be a big flirt and I knew she really wasn't. How did I know? I found out from one of my close friends, who knew from one of her close friends, that Lolly Adams had been brought up in a Mormon family. That's not proof, of course, but close to it, because if she really had been brought up as a Mormon she would have been inundated with "No, no, no—you mustn't do this and you mustn't do that, because it's not proper for a young lady and it could lead to sin." But then why the hell does she put on that flirtatious act at every party where I happen to see her? Or at the screening of a foreign film at the Writers Guild? Or in Gelson's supermarket? Or at the Shubert Theatre on the opening night of the latest Broadway play to come to Los Angeles and which I'm reviewing?

I didn't actually know her name until Toby Pryce, my English friend, introduced us at a wedding: "Lolly Adams, let me introduce my dear friend Tom Cole." I found out later that "Lolly" was short for Loretta, but she preferred "Lolly" on all occasions.

The weather this May was unusually cool and yet Lolly

wore the most revealing dresses, which came close to the edge of indiscretion without actually falling in. For instance, her blackberry-colored organza dress, which I saw at a charity ball for Kids in Crisis last Sunday at the Hotel Bel-Air, was something like a peek-a-boo contest that showed her naked legs underneath that dress—only for a second—and then if she made the slightest movement, this enticing burlesque show was suddenly gone with the wind. Well, she knew what she was doing . . . if intrigue was her plan.

Since everyone was dancing or drinking in that romantically decorated ballroom, I decided to demystify this Gypsy Rose Lee imitator. I asked Lolly to dance with me. Without hesitation, she put down her drink, put up her arms, and pressed her warm cheek against mine.

"I was hoping you'd ask," she said, and off we went.

The orchestra was playing a pretty song that sounded familiar, but I couldn't remember the title. Lolly began singing in my ear: "And when we're dancing and you're dangerously near me, I get ideas . . . I get ideas." she sang in a whisper.

I wasn't sure what she was trying to do, seduce me or tease me, as her warm breath raised the temperature in my ear and other parts of my body.

"Are you talking to me?" I asked stupidly.

"Those are the lyrics, dear. I've always liked that old song."

I felt like a fool. While I was holding her sultry body

and we were still dancing cheek to cheek, I tried to recover my composure.

"Do you come here oft—No, I mean—we seem to bump into each other all over the place, don't we?"

"Yes, I've planned it that way," she said.

"Now wait a second—are you serious?" I couldn't see her eyes, only her right ear, which protruded through her black hair and rubbed against my nose.

"Of course," she said. "I call that magazine you write for and ask them to tell me which plays, movies, weddings and charity balls you're scheduled to attend."

I pulled my cheek away and looked at her eyes, which were twinkling as if she had just told a wonderful joke. My God her beautiful black hair goes so well with that blackberry-colored dress and the white pearl necklace she's wearing.

"I don't know what to make of you, Lolly."

"You will, dear . . . just takes a little time."

Half an hour later, I escorted Lolly across the small stone bridge that covered the lagoon surrounding much of Hotel Bel-Air. Two magnificent white swans were gliding effortlessly in the water below us. Lolly stopped walking and took my arm.

"Look—aren't they lovely, Tom? They're always together. I love to watch them whenever I come here."

This was a side of the flirtatious lady that I hadn't

expected. We left the swans and walked to the valet parking attendants who were only a dozen feet away. We gave them our parking tickets.

"Well, I suppose you know my next move, Lolly."

"I never presume, Tom—it only leads to disappointment."

"No, I meant about my work schedule. You said my magazine tells you all my moves and exactly where I'm going to be."

"Oh, I don't look at schedules anymore; I prefer surprises," she said with a precocious smile. "It's more exhilarating."

"Lolly, may I ask what you do for a living?"

"I'm a dressmaker—part of the time," she answered.

"Seriously?"

"Of course," she answered with a soft smile.

"Did you make the dress you're wearing tonight?" I asked.

"Of course. Do you like it?"

"Well, it's very original," I said.

"But do you like it?"

"I think it's fascinating," I said, which was certainly true.

"But do you like it?" she insisted.

"Yes, I do," I said.

"Good! Here come our cars."

One of the valets drove up with Lolly's white Infiniti. My gray Toyota Camry followed behind. As her valet opened the door for Lolly, I put out my hand.

"Good night, Lolly."

"Ar-en-cha going to give me a little good-night kiss?" she asked, with only the hint of a smile.

An impulse bypassed my brain and went directly into my arms. I pulled her body into mine and kissed her on the lips for at least ten seconds. The valet watched with an envious smile.

"That's better," she said. She gave the valet a five-dollar tip, got into her car, and drove away . . . leaving me in a daze.

The following Thursday evening I was assigned to cover the opening-night revival of the Rodgers & Hammerstein musical *Oklahoma!* I had heard that this production was wonderful, but my job, of course, was to give my own opinion, not what I heard.

The Shubert Theatre was filling up quickly. I had my regular eighth-row center seat. With notebook and pen in hand, I glanced every now and then to see if Mademoiselle Flirt was walking down any of the aisles, but there was no sign of her as the house lights began to dim. I sat back and relaxed, hoping to be entertained.

The overture was wonderful, the curtain went up, and the audience gave an audible sigh of remembrance when Curly began singing, "Oh, what a beautiful morning."

When the adorable character of Ado Annie made her entrance—which I think the entire audience was anticipating—I watched with puzzlement. After a few words of dialogue, and despite her country accent, I realized that I was watching Lolly. The unexpectedness of it hit me like an electric shock: Lolly Adams playing a country hick. It seemed inconceivable. So that's what she meant by "I'm a dressmaker—*part of the time.*"

I hoped with all my heart that when she began singing I wouldn't cringe, because I had to review Lolly. Of course, I could just leave out any mention of Ado Annie, but that would be completely unprofessional.

The orchestra gave her a slight introduction, she opened her mouth, and out came a glorious voice. A showstopper.

> I'm just a girl who cain't say no,
>> I'm in a terrible fix,
> I always say "come on, let's go!"
>> Jist when I orta say nix.

The audience loved her . . . and how appropriate the lyrics were.

During the intermission I looked at the Who's Who in the Playbill. There she was:

Ado Annie, played by the delightful Lolly Adams, revives the role that brought her to the attention of critics and producers in the Broadway revival of *Oklahoma!* three years ago. Lolly was Elsie B. Hunter's understudy and took over the role of Ado Annie when Ms. Hunter discovered that she was with child.

When the final act curtain came down, the audience roared their approval. The cast got seven curtain calls and the loudest roar went up when Lolly took her solo bow.

This whole thing was getting curiouser and curiouser.

As the packed house was slowly shuffling through the aisles, anxious to go to their late-night suppers, I debated whether it was proper for me to go backstage to see Lolly.

Why not, I said to myself. *No!* I answered. *It's very unprofessional for a critic who's going to review the show to go backstage and talk with one of the actors. But I want to see her so shut up,* I finally told myself.

I went backstage and up a flight of stairs. I asked some costume person where Ms. Adams's dressing room was.

"She's in the third door down, sir."

I walked to her dressing room door with my heart pounding a little faster than normal. As I was about to knock, I saw a note pinned onto the door. It was written with pen and ink on custom-designed white paper:

THE EARLY BIRD CATCHES THE WORM

I knocked on her door several times, thinking that she was just playing one of her games again, but after my third or fourth knock one of the actors, who walked by on his way out, said, "Lolly left quite a while ago, sir."

I wrote my review of *Oklahoma!* on my notepad and phoned it in. As perturbed as I was with her "early bird catches the worm" note, I gave the show—and especially Lolly—a rave review. As I walked to my car, I couldn't get that damned note on the door out of my mind.

The next morning I searched through my telephone book for twenty minutes.

Adams, Lolly: Los Angeles	Dressmakers: Beverly Hills
Adams, Lolly: Beverly Hills	Dressmakers: Century City
Adams, Lolly: Westwood	Dressmakers: West Hollywood
Adams, Lolly: Hollywood	Dressmakers: Hollywood

THAT'S ENOUGH! Let her find me if she's so damn smart. *She's* the flirt, not me. I threw all my telephone books against the wall and knocked over my brand new Black & Decker toaster oven. If it's ruined, *she* should pay for it.

"Now let's be smart," I said to myself. "Stay calm. Don't let that silly flirt turn you into an idiot. You can be just as clever as she is, so relax! No matter how cute and beguiling and frustratingly voluptuous she is, don't let her drive you crazy! That's what she wants, don't you see?" All right! I'll show that snooty flirt who's cleverer.

I decided to go to the theater again, get up *before* the curtain comes down, stand in the hallway in front of her dressing room door, and wait for her before she can even go in.

That evening I got out of my seat before any of the curtain calls, walked swiftly up the aisle and through the stage door entrance, bounced up to the second floor and stood guard outside her dressing room. I couldn't help smiling as I anticipated the look on her face when she saw me.

I heard applause, and then the roar that must have been Lolly's solo bow. It wouldn't be long now. Actors and wardrobe personnel came rushing up the stairs and disappearing into the row of dressing rooms. A very tall bald man walked up to Lolly's door and started to walk into her room.

"Excuse me," I said before he could enter. "I believe that's Lolly Adams's dressing room."

"Yes, we changed just before the show," he said. "Her air-conditioning unit wasn't working and I offered my smaller room because it was nice and cool."

"That was very kind of you," I said with a twisted smile. "Where is your dressing room, if I may ask?"

"It's on the third floor, sir . . . number fourteen, end of the hall."

I thanked him, rushed up the stairs, and ran to room 14. When I got there, a little out of breath, I saw a note on the door.

IF AT FIRST YOU DON'T SUCCEED
TRY, TRY AGAIN

That little bitch. She's just playing with me. I went to bed that night and tried to sleep, but this snooty, voluptuous flirt was driving me crazy. I just couldn't get her under her skin. No, I mean—I couldn't *not* get her under *my* skin. No, that's not good English. I mean . . . oh, shut up and go to sleep.

Sitting pathetically by myself on Saturday evening, drinking my third glass of Pinot Grigio at a little bistro that I often frequented, I reasoned this way: Why go to the theater again? She'll just leave another clever note for me to choke on. If she's performing every night at the Shubert Theatre she must be free on Sunday nights, and surely she would want to go out somewhere, to some happy place where she could drink and dance and flirt with all the men.

Where would she go this Sunday? There's an open-air celebration after the last performance of Cirque de Soleil. But what if it rains?

There's also the grand opening of Nobu's new restaurant in the building that used to be L'Orangerie . . . possibly, Nobu might have live music, but I doubt if he would have dancing.

There's going to be a twentieth wedding anniversary reception for Leonard and Susan Nimoy tomorrow night at the Hotel Bel-Air, and I was invited. And she loves those swans.

I wore my tuxedo, just in case the other men wore tuxedos. It was still early when I arrived and not many guests were there.

The small orchestra was playing Schumann quintets.

Leonard was in a tuxedo, along with two or three men who were good friends with the anniversary couple, but the other men at the party were wearing suits. After I said my hellos to the Nimoys, I walked around the ballroom to see if I could find Ms. Hot Tamale, but she wasn't there. Within fifteen or twenty minutes I gave up the search.

When the orchestra switched to old standards, people began walking to the dance floor and hugging each other as they danced. My feelings of loneliness are a little vulnerable when I'm alone and hear nostalgic music, so I decided to slip out quietly before I felt too sorry for myself.

It was a beautiful night: stars, moonlight, and not much wind. I walked over the little bridge that spanned the lagoon and stopped to see if there was a swan in sight. I did see one in the shadows; his or her body shone brightly as it floated into the moonlight. I watched for a while and then heard "Tweet, tweet, tweet" behind me. I turned and saw Lolly. She was wearing a very discreet silk and lace white gown. She could almost have been one of those beautiful white swans.

"You're early," she said. "I didn't think you'd get here so soon."

"The early bird catches the worm, you know," I said, "which is very smart if you happen to like eating worms."

She didn't smirk at my stupid joke; she only stared at me with the sweetest suggestion of a smile. As I looked at the moonlight reflected in her eyes I felt oddly helpless.

She just stood there, watching me, and waiting. For what? I suddenly threw all my thoughts into the lagoon and put my arms around her body. She moved into my embrace as if we were dancing and I kissed her tenderly, again and again, and then so passionately that tears began dripping down her cheeks.

"I've chased you for such a long time, Tom . . . and now you've finally caught me," she whispered.

Really
Are You ^ in Love

I asked Melanie to marry me when she came to my house for dinner. Her mother came with her. I didn't know Melanie that well, but I knew I was really in love with her. She was so much fun to be with and so pretty. I knew I wanted to marry her. I asked my mother to give me a ring. She got one from a cereal box and I put it on Melanie's finger and then I kissed her. Melanie just giggled. I was three and a half years old.

We had a Christmas party the next week and Melanie was invited. When she walked into our house she wanted to hug me, but I didn't even talk to her because I wanted to play with my new truck. Melanie asked if she could play with me, but I just shoved her away.

My name is Joey Singer. I wonder how different I am now, thirty-five years later, from the way I was then. Do you think this is a ridiculous question, dear reader?

On a hot July morning at five o'clock I got a call from the American director of a film I'd written. It was being shot in France.

"Joey, I need you to come to Paris immediately if not

sooner, and rewrite those two big scenes inside the château and I'm going nuts and I have to shoot them next week. Can you come right away? Please? I'll be your best friend."

I got on a plane a few hours later.

On my first day of work I met Ann Goursaud, who was French, spoke English perfectly, and was chief editor on the film. Ann and the director and I worked every day from 10:00 a.m. till 6:00 p.m.

Ann really knew her onions about editing and she gave the director some wonderful suggestions about what was wrong and what she thought I should rewrite in those difficult scenes. She offered her suggestions strongly but humbly, always looking at the director as she said, "But of course, it's your film," and then she would wink at me. I liked Ann very much. I asked if she was married or attached. When she said no, I asked her to have dinner with me that first night.

We took a taxi to a bistro she loved, Chez Allard, which served delicious country food that I'd never eaten or heard of before. The waiters were used to speaking English to American, English, and German tourists, but when they saw Ann they spoke in French. Ann translated for me. We shared warm sausages over cabbage and steamed potatoes for a starter, and then guinea hen for two. The wine they served was a little expensive but delicious. The elderly man who was serving us referred to the wine as "honest."

After dinner we stepped outside and found that the night was warm but not as sultry as earlier, so we took a long walk to the Eiffel Tower. When we got there I saw a young man,

North African, I think, who was selling ice cream cones from his small cart on wheels. Ann and I each picked pistachio and sat on a bench directly under the great Eiffel Tower. We ate our ice cream cones and tried to guess the different languages we were hearing as people passed by.

Ann had to get up the next morning much earlier than I did. As she was about to enter the taxi I hailed for her, she gave me one of those polite little kisses on each cheek, in the French style, and then started to get into the taxi. I pulled her back, very gently, and gave her a long, tender kiss. She stared at me for several seconds without saying anything, and then gave the driver her address. We had dinner together every night after that for the rest of the week.

The next night Ann showed me Montmartre, which was packed with tourists. A very colorfully dressed woman was playing romantic French songs on her accordion. Just what I needed.

An artist made a silhouette of Ann using a small piece of black paper and a scissors. It was a good likeness. An elderly fortune-teller, wearing a beret and tennis shoes, looked at my left palm—for which I paid him one euro—and then said that I was an artist from the tip of my toes to the top of my head and that I would live to be ninety-two. I was very pleased with my fortune, of course, until a few minutes later when we passed the old man again. He was talking to an English teenager, whose parents were standing next to the boy listening to their son's fortune. All I heard was "live to be ninety-two."

The week that Ann and I were together, day and night, was the happiest week of my life. I was falling in love. When it was time for me to leave Ann and France it was difficult to say good-bye. I said I'd call her regularly and promised that we would see each other soon.

A few weeks after the film was finished, and after getting a recommendation from our director, Ann was offered her first job on a film that was going to be shot in Los Angeles. A low-budget film, but they wanted her. She almost choked with excitement as she told me the details on the telephone. When I met her at the Los Angeles airport, she jumped into my arms and wrapped her legs around my waist.

We lived together in the small house I had rented near Paramount Pictures. Sweet days and nights followed, without any hidden rancor and no silent chip on her shoulder if I did something small and stupid. She was always cheerful and loving, and I think we laughed every day.

The next months were *almost* wonderful, except that word was getting out about how remarkable an editor she was. Ann was becoming known and respected as a chief editor and was in demand.

When the low-budget film she had been working on in Los Angeles was finished, she asked if I would mind if she took a six-week job on location in Tucson, Arizona, before the filming continued in Los Angeles. The director was supposed to be very talented, but this would be his first film and the studio wanted Ann to work with him while he was on location, to make sure he wouldn't get into technical difficulties or waste a lot of money.

"If you say no I won't go—I'll just stay with you," she said with a smile, and I believe she meant it.

"I'll miss you to pieces," I said, "but your work comes first . . . always . . . as long as it's not more than six weeks. And if I get lonely I'll cry for only a day or two and then I'll pay you a surprise visit." Ann sat on my lap and hugged me.

We talked to each other on the telephone almost every evening at nine o'clock, except during night shooting. But three weeks after she got on the plane for Tucson with the cast and crew, I discovered that I was angry with her for leaving me alone. It was an ugly realization, and stupid. I yelled at myself in the mirror, calling myself vile names for being such a baby, then picked up the phone and made a reservation to fly to Tucson the next afternoon.

I landed at Tucson International Airport at five o'clock on a Thursday afternoon. It was still hot and humid, but the sun was starting to ease up as it made its way west.

Ann was staying at the Arizona Inn, which she had told me was a beautiful hotel and resort, with a swimming pool and two clay tennis courts. I walked into the small, quietly elegant lobby and asked the gentleman at the reception desk to please ring Ann's room.

"Ms. Goursaud left town yesterday with the movie crew, sir. They're in Johnsonville. She said she'd be back on Sunday evening or Monday."

"Did she leave a message for me? My name is Joey Singer."

The receptionist looked in box 207.

"No, sir, I'm sorry. No message."

"But . . . well, is it all right if I stay in her room tonight? I came a long way to see her," I said with a confident laugh.

"Did she know you were coming?"

"No, I was going to surprise her."

"I'm sorry, sir, but if she didn't tell any of us about your coming, I'm afraid we can't do that. Perhaps you'd like another room?"

"Yes," I said, somewhat flustered.

"Single or suite, sir?"

"I don't know . . . well, yes, a suite, please."

"Yes, sir. Would you like to be near the pool?

"It doesn't matter. Wait, all right—near the pool. That'll be fine."

The clerk gave me a key, which was attached to a large wooden knob so that you wouldn't take it by mistake. When I said that I didn't need any help carrying my small overnight bag I was given directions to my room.

I walked along a small stone path to suite 109. I noticed that the path was bordered on each side by impatiens and pansies, which I would have appreciated more if my brain hadn't been racing a mile a minute. Why didn't she let me know? Not fair to me. And it's not like her. Oh, Jesus . . . not a location romance. How many times have I seen it?

Only every time I've been on location, doing rewrites. It's epidemic with movie crews. With the guys it's one week away from home and they suddenly get the seven-year itch: "One or two nights with that cute script girl—nothing serious." With the gals it's "Maybe one night with that handsome son-uv-a-bitch assistant director who hollers at the crew but keeps flirting with me." Oh, yes . . . I know all about location romances.

Suite 109 was very nice, with a king-size bed and small framed watercolors of 1920s ladies and gentlemen playing tennis. The women wore long dresses and hats; the men were in white trousers, wearing long-sleeved rolled-up shirts, which must have been very uncomfortable.

I decided to take a swim before dinner to try to clear my head of anger and frustration and all my stupid thoughts. I hadn't brought a swimming suit, but, what the hell, my blue boxer shorts would fool anyone who might still be at the pool. Two bathrobes were hanging on wall knobs in the bathroom and large towels were spread over towel racks.

The pool was only about thirty yards from my suite. I saw two people there: an elderly gentleman, who was just wiping himself off and getting into his sandals, and a woman who was lying on a lounge chair, reading. She had short, curly blond hair and was wearing those oversized sunglasses and a visor. She was also wearing a very revealing bikini, if that isn't an oxymoron. I put my towel down on a lounge chair near hers. She looked up and lowered her sunglasses when she saw me.

"Good book?" I asked.

"The usual cheap junk," she answered. "Sex and violence."

"Why do you read it?" I asked.

"I like it. Doesn't require any brain power."

As I took off my robe and got ready to enter the pool, I noticed that she was giving me the once-over. Maybe she perceived that I was wearing thin boxer underwear instead of a bathing suit. Well, at least somebody's glad I'm here.

"My name is Estelle," the almost naked woman said before I got into the water. "What's yours?" she asked.

Careful . . . careful, I told myself. *You never know.*

"Jimmy!" I hollered back as I jumped into the pool and swam six laps.

While I was breast-stroking back and forth across the pool I wondered if the bikini would still be there when I came out. I guessed that she would. When I finished my laps and got out, there she was, standing up and gathering all of her paraphernalia into a colorful bag with leather handles.

"Are you here alone, Jimmy?"

"Just for tonight, actually," I said as I toweled off. "My girlfriend should be here tomorrow."

"What's her name?"

"Uh . . . Ann. She's working on a film here. Well, near here, I think. But she'll be back tomorrow. Maybe even tonight, for all I know. They're on location right now."

"They're in Johnsonville, aren't they?" Estelle asked with a little smile.

I was nonplussed. "How did you know that?" I asked.

"I heard one of the fellows—I think he was the transportation captain—telling his drivers the route they were supposed to take. He said they'd be coming back in three days."

Oh, dear, I thought I said to myself, but Estelle heard me say it.

"That's terrible for you," she said. "I'm so sorry. Would you like to have dinner with me tonight? I'm all alone, too, for a little while, anyway. How 'bout dinner right here at the inn . . . an early night. Whaddya say?"

"Well . . . okay. Sure. That's very nice of you."

Estelle lingered over her packing. She seemed to be looking at my wet undershorts, which I quickly covered with a towel.

"Is seven thirty all right for you, Jimmy?" she said as she walked away.

"Fine," I said.

"See you in the dining room."

"Why don't you call me Essie?" Estelle asked while we were both eating our shrimp cocktail, with white wine for me and a gin martini for her. "Everyone calls me that."

"All right, Essie," I said a little hesitantly.

The dining room had a friendly, sand-colored interior

with several paintings of Indian chiefs on the walls. There were only a handful of people still eating or about to eat. Essie was wearing a halter dress that was remarkably low cut.

"Why did you tell me your name was Jimmy? It's really Joey, isn't it?"

Uh-oh. You're a writer—think fast, pal. "Well, my dad always used to call me Jimmy because he and Mom lost a son . . . they were going to name him Jimmy. I was only two years old then, but my dad always called me Jimmy after that. It just sort of stuck."

Maybe it was my imagination, but Essie smiled at me as if she were saying, "Fast thinker." Or maybe it was "stinker."

We had both ordered lamb chops and shared a bottle of Chianti. When our food arrived Essie raised her glass: "Live, love, and be happy—that's my motto," she exclaimed, too loudly I thought.

"Yes," I repeated, like a chimpanzee who could both mimic gestures and speak English. We clicked glasses.

When we finished dinner, Essie said: "Come on, I'll walk you home."

I gave a lecture to myself as Essie and I walked back along the path that led to my suite: *Now let's get something straight . . . I am not an adulterer! Essie isn't married—which she made very clear to me during dinner—and I'm not married, I'm just in love. So adultery doesn't even enter into this situation. Betrayal? Yes . . . but who has betrayed whom? To be really in love with someone who runs off for six weeks—which is fine, I understand that—but she didn't even let me know that she was going to another town, when she certainly might have guessed that the surprise visit I told her I was going to make, after crying from loneliness for three weeks, would be—*

"Penny for your thoughts," Essie said, interrupting my mental conversation.

"I was . . . thinking about Ann, actually."

"How terribly frustrated you must feel after making a wonderful surprise visit and then finding out that's she's gone," she said.

"Well . . . something like that," I said, wondering if she was a spider talking to a fly.

"I have a remedy for you," she said.

"Uh-oh—I mean, oh?"

"Would you like to hear my remedy?" she asked.

"Sure!"

"Why don't we have one lovely fuck, just to get all of that useless frustration out of your system, so you can be yourself again, calm and happy, when your beloved comes back?"

I stood like a dummy, listening to my brain and then to my body.

No, yes, no, YESSSSS, no, YESSSSSSSS . . . no.

"I know how to handle you, Joey, so that all of that terrible frustration will just stream out of you like a burst dam."

"Well . . . all right."

"What did you say, dear?"

"I said, all right. That might just be the sink that thinks me."

It was quick all right, and she knew exactly what she was doing—even providing condoms. I think she had a drawer full. It was like making love in a pharmacy. She was the frustrated one—probably a nympho—and she appealed to my basest self. She was out and gone after fifteen minutes, and I did not feel relieved, I felt disgusted with myself. I made a reservation to fly back to Los Angeles on the ten a.m. flight the next morning and wished with all my heart that Ann would never find out about the disgraceful thing I had done. I thought I was getting a little toy to play with in my loneliness, but instead I received a visit from the devil.

When I got home I took another shower, my fourth one . . . three last night and another as soon as I walked into my home. As I was toweling off I listened to my messages.

> *My sweet darling, They changed our schedule because one of the actors got sick and we all have to leave tonight at eight p.m. I've tried calling you three times but there wasn't any answer. Where were you? Did they make you work late at the studio?*
>
> *We're going to a little town called Johnsonville, which is God knows where. The operator at the*

*Arizona Inn promised me that she would read this
message to you as soon as you called, and she even
instructed another operator to read it when she went
off duty. Our director is giving me off for the
weekend, so I'll see you Saturday afternoon. I don't
want you to be too lonely.*

*Good night, my sweetheart. I love you and long
for you so much it hurts.*

I kept hitting my head against the wall until I heard a
key in the door and saw Ann walk in.

"Darling," I hollered in a panic-stricken, squeaky voice.
"What a wonderful surprise."

Ann stared at me, stoically, as she glanced at the towel
around my waist, which was the only thing I was wearing.

"I just listened to your message . . . only just this minute," I said.

Ann didn't come any closer. She just stared at me with
cold eyes.

"Is this your work outfit?" she asked. "Or is this something Essie picked out for you?"

Oh dear god in heaven please help me.

"I'm leaving you, Joey. I'll pack up my things and be
gone in half an hour. All I ask is that you don't start ex-
plaining."

"Wait, wait, honey, please. I love you. Don't do this. Please
forgive me. Don't leave me, darling. Please. I don't want to
live without you. It wasn't love or desire, it was—"

"I DON'T WANT TO KNOW WHAT IT WAS OR WASN'T—I'M LEAVING YOU! Tú est un con, tú comprend?"

"But where will you go?" I cried out as she walked into our bedroom.

"None of your fucking business! That is your business, isn't it?" she said as she slammed the bedroom door.

I sat on the sofa, quietly going crazy. How could this happen? I was only three and a half years old. I didn't know any better, Melanie. I want to marry you . . . I gave you a ring, remember? Please forgive me . . . I'll let you play with my truck. I'm just a stupid little boy. Don't leave me, Melanie. Please don't leave me. I really love you.

My Old Flame

In 1983 Buddy Silberman was in Milwaukee, Wisconsin, having dinner with the Silberman family and a few of his old friends.

When he finished eating, joking, and laughing, he got lonely. He couldn't get his old girlfriend, Shirley, out of his mind, ever since his Aunt Clarabelle said at dinner, "Buddy, I bumped into your old flame yesterday. She's coloring hair on Capitol Drive . . . a new place called Lovely to Look At."

Buddy hadn't seen Shirley for three and a half years, after he "sort of" dumped her. Shirley wasn't a beauty or a knock-out or a "honey"; she was a simple, very pleasant, ordinary girl with ordinary brownish hair and an attractive body. He liked her, but not in the way that she cared for him. He was never in love with Shirley—or anyone else, for that matter—he was just in sex with her.

But as long as I'm back in Milwaukee for a few days, what the hell—why not give Shirley a call? he said to himself. *See if she's married or something.*

He looked up the telephone number of the beauty parlor and dialed. When he heard Shirley's voice, he said:

"Hey, good lookin', what's new?"

"Who is this?"

"Buddy Silberman! Remember me?—the tall, good-lookin' guy you used to have a crush on a few years ago?"

"Where are you?" Shirley asked with an unfriendly tone in her voice.

"I'm in Milwaukee. I came all this way to see if you were married or if you're still a honey."

"Who died?"

"Whaddya mean? Nobody died."

"Then why are you here?" Shirley asked.

"Well—I had a little business and thought I could kill two birds with one stone."

"And I'm one of the birds?" Shirley asked.

"No, no—I mean—come on, Shirley. I just wondered if I could get to see you if you were free tonight, and if you still liked me and wouldn't mind a porterhouse steak and the best bottle of wine you've ever had since you saw me last."

"Are you looking to shtup me tonight, Buddy?"

"Now, Shirley, be fair. I'm trying to pay you compliments and you're throwing hot coals at me. Don't you know when I'm trying to be funny? You always used to."

"You haven't changed much, Buddy."

"Oh yeah, I have. I promise you. I moved to L.A. and grew up a little. I'm a smarter and deeper schmuck than I was before. And I get lonely when I think about you. Is that so terrible?"

After a long pause, Shirley said, "There's lots of people waiting to be colored. I've got to get back to them, Buddy."

"Can't I please see you again, Shirley? I really do miss you . . . and the steak is real good . . . ?"

Silence for a moment. Then Shirley said, "I wonder if you have changed."

"Does that mean yes for the porterhouse?"

"You're not going to hurt my feelings again, are you, Buddy?"

"Opposite."

After another pause, Shirley said, "I get off at six, but I want to go home first and shower and get dressed and everything. You can pick me up at seven. Where did you want to go?"

"I thought the Tuscany steak house, if you still like that place?" Buddy asked.

"That's fine. I'll see you at seven. I'm in the same house, Buddy."

"See ya later, alligator," Buddy answered.

True to his word, Buddy ordered a twenty-two-ounce porterhouse steak for two, plus a bottle of Château Magdalena, his new favorite wine and one of the only wines he could remember the name of. He and Shirley each had a "Martini of Shrimp," which was just a shrimp cocktail served in a martini glass, and they both ate their shrimp with Absolut vodka.

"Like old times, Shirley."

"I'm happy you called, Buddy—if only it could stay this way."

"If 'ifs' and 'buts' were candy and nuts, the world would be a fruit tree," Buddy said, as if he had just made up his little saying on the spur of the moment.

"That's what you used to say to me four years ago," Shirley said, not unkindly, but with an ironic smile.

"Oh well, I still feel the same way," Buddy answered.

"About me or the candy and nuts?" Shirley asked.

"Both. I'm a poet, Shirley. That's my way of expressing my feelings about you." Buddy reached over and held Shirley's free hand.

When the sommelier arrived and poured a little wine into a glass for Buddy to test, Buddy said, "This beautiful lady is my wine sommel whatcha call it. Let her decide if it's any good."

The sommelier offered the glass to Shirley. When she took a sip, her eyes lit up.

"This'll be fine," Shirley said to the sommelier. She took Buddy's hand and said quietly, "Buddy, this is a wonderful wine. Thank you."

Their steak arrived. It had been carved into perfectly even slices, going from medium to rare. Shirley's face was filled with awe after her first bite.

"I haven't eaten meat like this in a long time, Buddy."

"Stick with me, kid." Buddy said as he chewed on a mouthful of steak and asparagus au gratin.

When they finished eating the steak, Buddy asked,

"What do you like for dessert, Shirley—the Cherries Jubilee? You used to love that."

"I couldn't eat any more, Buddy. I'm stuffed and everything was delicious. Just a cup of coffee would be great."

"Me, too. Don't wanna get too full. Not tonight," Buddy said with a smile and a little wink.

Buddy pulled up to Shirley's house in his rented Cadillac. When she opened the front door and stepped into her living room, Buddy started to follow, but Shirley stopped him.

"Not tonight, Buddy."

"Wait a minute! What happened? Did I do something wrong?"

"No. Tonight you didn't do anything wrong. I just want to remember how lovely this evening has been, in case I never see you again."

"But . . ."

"Good night, Buddy. Thank you again." Shirley gave Buddy a quick kiss on the cheek, went into her house, and shut the door.

For twenty or thirty seconds, Buddy stood next to his rented Cadillac, trying to understand what had happened. He felt as if he had just seen a French film without subtitles.

A week later, in Los Angeles, Buddy and Sonny were having lunch at Junior's delicatessen.

"You're morose, Buddy."

"I'm not a moron and don't ever say that to me again."

"I didn't call you a moron, you jerk. I just wondered why you were so sad today."

"I got some strange thoughts running though my head that you don't know anything about, Sonny." Buddy took a sip of his Dr. Brown's cream soda as his eyes drifted off into space.

"Well, you'll feel better if you tell me about those strange thoughts. I'm your friend—talk to me!"

"It's about my old girlfriend, Shirley."

"The girl from Milwaukee?" Sonny asked.

"Yeah. My old flame," Buddy said quietly, as he took a bite of his corned beef sandwich.

"What's up?" Sonny asked.

"I am. I'm up in the air. I saw Shirley last week and got that old feeling again. We had a nice time, but she wouldn't come across. She said I hurt her feelings when I dumped her four years ago and she doesn't want to go through that again."

"You blame her for that?" Sonny asked.

"No, that's the trouble. I blame myself for being such a moron. She's a good girl and very sweet and always kind to everyone and we always had a nice time together . . . and then I screwed up. Now I've lost her."

"Are you in love, Buddy?"

"How the hell would I know?" Buddy said angrily.

"Well, Buddy—I'm the one who can help you," Sonny said with authority.

"Thank you, doctor. Start helping."

"Why don't you invite her out here? You pay for the trip, spend a little time with her, take her to some nice restaurants, stay at your apartment a lot, and see what it's like to be alone with her. Cook with her and watch TV together. Maybe that way you can see how deep the water is."

"You're smart," Buddy said. "You are a smart son of a bitch, Sonny."

"Coming from you, that's almost a compliment," Sonny replied.

"I got an idea," Buddy said, as if lightning had just struck. "What if I tell her that I suddenly got an opening in my schedule and how about if she came out and visited me and stayed at my place, just for a week, and I'll pay for everything—tickets and everything—and I'll take her to nice restaurants and make her as happy as a clam? I don't know why the hell clams should be so happy, but it sounds good. Whaddya think, Sonny?"

"You hit the jackpot, kid."

That night, the telephone rang in Sonny's apartment.

"Sonny Hurwitz speaking."

"It worked," Buddy said with a rare burst of excitement in his voice. "She's coming here this Saturday and she's gonna stay till next Saturday."

"Congratulations. Now get some plants and flowers and spread them all around your living room and bedroom. Maybe even in the kitchen."

"In the kitchen? What for?"

"To make your apartment seem romantic instead of looking like a betting parlor for football and horse races. And turn off the television set in your bedroom when she arrives."

"Okay, you're the doctor. I hope this works," Buddy said and hung up.

Five days later Buddy called Sonny from a drugstore.

"Sonny Hurwitz speaking."

"I'm goin' nuts."

"What's the matter?" Sonny asked. "You said everything was hunky-dory."

"The first night, yes," Buddy said with some desperation in his voice. "But now I can't get rid of her."

"But this is just Tuesday. She doesn't leave until Saturday."

"I KNOW IT—THAT'S WHAT'S DRIVING ME NUTS!" Buddy shrieked.

"All right, all right! Calm down and tell me what seems to be wrong."

Buddy took a few deep breaths and then started calmly.

"I got brand-new tubes of Colgate toothpaste . . . she uses Arm and Hammer. I wanna see Bruce Willis in a *Die Hard* flick and she wants to see *Little Women*. I like to watch television at least till one a.m. She wants to go to sleep, with lights out, at ten thirty. I like coffee in the morning, she likes tea. I like steak and chops for dinner, she like fish most of the time. Beef is okay, but just once in a while, she says. I tell ya—I gotta get her out of here or I'll have a conniption."

Sonny thought for a while before answering.

"Who invited her, Buddy?"

"Yeah, yeah, yeah! I knew you were gonna say that. So what? You want me to go crazy?" Buddy asked, as if he were the most reasonable man in the world.

"No," Sonny answered softly. "I want you to be the decent, compassionate gentleman that I know you can be."

"Yes, Mama. I'll be a good boy. I'll just tell her that someone died in Florida and I have to—"

"No, no. None of that stuff," Sonny said. "You can be a gentleman for three more days, it won't kill you. But don't hurt that girl again, Buddy. You mustn't hurt her again."

Sonny's words got to Buddy. He was a gentleman, with heartburn, for three more days. On Saturday, he took Shirley to the airport for her 10:00 a.m. flight to Milwaukee. When it came time to say good-bye, Shirley looked at him with soft compassion in her eyes.

"I know my visit was difficult for you, Buddy."

"What're you talkin' about?" Buddy answered, as if he had never heard of anything so absurd in his life. "It was a joy. You know I'm a little nuts sometimes, Shirley. I think business worries got to me and I think I took it out on you once in a while. But I loved every minute you were here."

"You told me once that you never lie," Shirley said softly. "Don't start now. It was one of the things I admired most about you. Most people lie all the time."

Buddy didn't or couldn't answer. He looked away from

Shirley's eyes like a puppy who knows it has done a bad thing.

Shirley leaned over and kissed him gently on the cheek. "Thank you for a wonderful time," she said, then turned and walked down the ramp to her plane.

Three months passed. This time someone in Milwaukee *did* die—Buddy's oldest school chum and fellow gambler, Lenny Fisher. Buddy decided to go to the funeral.

While he was packing his suitcase, the memory of Shirley passed through Buddy's mind several times, quickly, but so pleasantly that the memory reached his heart. *Why not call her while I'm in Milwaukee?* he thought. *Either she wants to see me or she says get lost. All right, I wouldn't blame her if she did. But I want to see her. No porterhouse steak and wine baloney—I really do want to see her again. And I'll tell her I'm not lying—not to her or myself.*

Buddy called the beauty parlor. His heart was thumping loudly as he waited for her to come to the phone. Then he heard her voice.

"This is Shirley."

"Shirley, this is Buddy Silberman."

"Buddy! What a surprise. Where are you?"

"I'm still in Los Angeles, but I'm leaving for Milwaukee today. This time somebody *did* die—my old friend Lenny Fisher."

"The fat man who smoked three packs a day?" Shirley asked.

"That's the schmuck. Fifty-eight years old. Anyway, I just want to let you know that I'll be in town for a few days, and—I don't know how to say this, but if—"

"Buddy, I'm married. Do you remember the man who owned a bicycle shop on Burleigh Street?"

"Near the Sherman movie theater . . . David somebody?" Buddy asked, trying to sound normal.

"That's right . . . Davey Putman. We went together for two months and then he suddenly popped the question. I really like him, Buddy. I mean, I love him, but I also like him so much, and I'm very happy."

"Well . . . I . . . I'm bursting with happiness for you, Shirley. The two of you should make a great couple, and . . . well . . . you'll finally learn how to ride a bicycle, won't you?"

"Yes, I will. I'd better go now. There's a whole crowd waiting for me to do their hair. Take care of yourself, Buddy."

"You bet," Buddy answered. He waited a few seconds after Shirley hung up and then slowly placed the phone back into its cradle.

The Anniversary

Today is September eighth . . . our seventeenth wedding anniversary. Diane and I were supposed to meet at six thirty at La Notte—our favorite restaurant in New York.

Maybe I arrived forty minutes early because I'm so anxious to give her the little anniversary present I bought for her. That's all right. No customers yet, so I have the whole place to myself. It's a nice feeling. The "whole place" is just twelve tables, which suits me fine. It's where Diane and I had our first date.

As soon as I entered, Nick, the owner, opened a bottle of Pinot Grigio, which he always has ready for us. He started to fill my wine glass.

"A little wine, Mr. Bellsey?"

"Just two drops, Nick. Let it get nice and cold."

"Certainly," he said, as he poured an inch or two of the Pinot Grigio and put the bottle into an ice bucket that was standing nearby.

I didn't want to drink very much before Diane got here. My surprise present is the delicate amethyst earrings that she admired weeks and weeks ago. I know that when she arrives she's going to rush up and give me a long kiss before she sits down. Then we'll click glasses, take a sip of wine, and say "Happy Anniversary, darling" at the same time. I'll hand her the present and wait for the look on her face when she sees that I remembered those earrings she admired so long ago.

Nick began to light tiny candles in the small glass holders that rested on each table. He wasn't Italian—although he pretended to be. He was actually Albanian, but he certainly knew what he was doing if it was romance he was selling. Each table also had a small chandelier above it, covered with faded orange lace. It gave the restaurant a warm glow.

As I took another sip of wine I heard the door open and looked to see if it was Diane, but it was the laundry service delivering clean napkins.

I looked at my watch: twelve minutes after six. It won't be long now, unless she's tied up at the hospital. She's a speech therapist specializing in aphasia, mostly for people who've suffered a stroke recently and have to learn how to talk again. She's awfully good at what she does. I think the way she speaks the English language is one of the things that attracted me to her. There were also one or two other things.

I drained the last few drops of wine in my glass. Nick snuck in quickly and gave me anther two inches of Pinot Grigio. I looked at my watch: six twenty. Ten more minutes—

she's never late. I began touching the real but very tiny fresh flowers that were in the miniature vase on my table.

On our first date she had long auburn hair. Now she has it cut much shorter and the auburn needs a little help from the beauty parlor, but I'm hoping she'll let it grow again this winter. That's a man's point of view, of course, but I fell in love with her when that beautiful hair framed her face.

The first time we made love she smiled almost the whole time. We had a small glass of port beforehand and lamb chops and Château Beychevelle after. I didn't find Diane until so late in my life, and now, seventeen years later, I honestly don't believe I could live without her.

The restaurant is beginning to fill up.

Each time the phone rings I'm afraid it's Diane, telling Nick that she's going to be late. But it's always someone who wants to make a reservation.

Twenty minutes till seven. It's not like her to be late, not without calling. Nick saw that I was getting anxious and rushed over.

"Would you like to order a little something, Mr. Bellsey?"

"Thank you, Nick. No, I'll wait till Mrs. Bellsey comes. I'm sure she won't be much longer."

Nick stared at me with frozen eyes.

"Are you . . . making a little joke, Mr. Bellsey?"

"No, what do you mean? Why would I joke just because

my wife is a little late? She'll be here soon, Nick, I promise . . . Why are you staring at me like that?"

"Because . . . I'm so sorry, Mr. Bellsey . . . I thought you were waiting for some friend. Please forgive me, but . . . Mrs. Bellsey died last year . . . on your anniversary . . . remember?"

I heard what he said, but I didn't understand.

Nick put his hand on my shoulder and stood next to me for several seconds, then left to greet an English couple who had just walked into the restaurant. Nick seated them a few tables away from me and walked to the back of the restaurant where he kept his CD recordings of Italian and Mexican piano music that his clients liked to hear while they ate. The first song he played was "Intermezzo." It was Diane's and my favorite . . . so romantic . . . first date . . .

Tears began to pour in my heart. I saw Nick looking at me and I wondered why he would do such a cruel thing, playing that particular sosng.

The English couple got up from their table and both of them hugged me.

"Haven't seen you since we got back from England. Sorry, Richard . . . both of us . . . We're going to miss her."

His wife kissed my cheek. "We loved her, Richard. She was a beautiful woman."

"Thank you," I said.

"We don't want to bother you—but if you *should* want to join us, just come right over."

After they went back to their table, Nick came over to me.

"I'm so sorry, Mr. Bellsey."

"Thank you, Nick."

I held his hand until he had to greet a party of four who were just walking in.

Tango Without Music

"I had a little haberdashery—shirts, ties, pants, you know—but when I started investing in real estate I made enough money to sort of retire."

A self-conscious silence ensued as Charley Sugarman brushed off imaginary crumbs from his clean white shirt. He sat nervously on the edge of a sofa, as if he were watching the final minutes of the Super Bowl.

"My wife says I have no sensitivity, so after twenty-three years she ups and leaves me."

Sugarman stared at Laura Bailey, a woman in her late forties with wild black hair, who was sitting in a large leather chair in colorful summer slacks, staring back at Charley Sugarman, waiting for him to speak.

"Okay . . . okay . . . my wife says I don't sing, I don't dance, I don't go to the theater, concerts, opera, or ballet, and she said that in the last eight years I've turned into an old codger. So now—would you please tell me what you think?"

"Does she want a divorce?" Laura Bailey asked.

"No, she doesn't want anything."

"Do you want a divorce, Mr. Sugarman?"

"No, I don't want a divorce. I love her."

"What's your wife's name?"

"Georgia."

"Where is she now, do you know?"

"She's staying at the Chesterfield Hotel for Women on East Sixty-third Street. Her father left her some money so she doesn't even ask me to pay. How do like that?"

"How do *you* like it?"

"I wanna know how *you* like it, Laura. I'm paying *you*, you're not paying me."

"All right, Charley—what do you want me to tell you?"

"I want you . . . to tell me . . . why, after twenty-three years of marriage, she walks out and leaves me all alone."

"Why do you think she left you?"

"I don't know. That's why I came to you."

"Well, if that's all you want to know, you're wasting your money. She's already told you why. She has a husband who isn't sensitive anymore and has started to act like an old codger. Seems clear to me."

"But . . . I mean, to leave me all alone . . . why would she want to hurt me this way? She never wanted to hurt me before."

"Probably because she loves you."

Tears started dripping down Sugarman's cheeks. He covered his face with his large freckled hands, as if he were ashamed that a grown man would cry in front of another person.

"Sit back, Mr. Sugarman. Please. You don't have to be embarrassed in front of me."

He sat back and wiped his eyes. His breathing slowed down.

"How old are you, Mr. Sugarman?"

"Fifty-three."

"That's not very old. Do you feel like an old codger?"

"Only from seven to ten in the morning and from seven to ten at night," Sugarman answered sarcastically.

"You think you're being cute, but I think you're actually telling me the truth. May I ask when you usually *don't* make love with your wife? . . . Seven to ten at night?"

Sugarman tried to talk, but the lump in his throat wouldn't allow words to come out. Finally, he spoke in a half whisper.

"Something seems to have dried up in me. Would you help me, because I'm lost? Please tell me what you think I should do."

"Do you dance, Mr. Sugarman?"

His voice suddenly came back loud and clear. "What the hell does that have to—Sorry! I'm sorry! Yes, I used to dance a little, but that was a long time ago."

"I want you to try something. I'm going to give you the address of the Ballard Studio, on Eighty-seventh and Broadway. I want you to take tango lessons."

"TANGO LESSONS? ARE YOU NUTS OR SOME—
Sorry! I'm sorry. Please forgive me. If that's what you want,
you're the doctor, Laura."

"I'm not a doctor, Charley."

"That's right, you're the other thing. Okay—Ballard Studio. Would you write it down for me, please?"

As she was writing the address, she said, "Ask for Antonio and tell him I sent you."

"How much do I owe you, Laura?"

"We'll see, Charley," she replied. "First take a few tango
lessons."

The next day, Sugarman called the Ballard Studio and asked
for Antonio. He waited nervously until the receptionist con-
nected him.

"Hullo, Antonio Rosa here."

"Hi, my name is Charles Sugarman. I'm . . . well, Laura
Bailey said I should ask for you."

"She is a very good friend. Please tell me what I can do
for you, Mr. Sugar."

"I just want to take a few tango lessons with you."

"For sure! When is good for you, Mr. Sugar?"

"It's Sugarman. Well—how about today? I mean, almost
any afternoon would be okay, but Mondays and Thursdays
are always good, if it's okay with you, Mr. Rosey."

"Today is fine. Three o'clock is good for you?"

"Yes, that's good."

"Okay! You know where my studio is?"

"Yes, I do! Laura wrote it down for me."

"Wonderful! I see you today at three. And by the way, you can call me Antonio."

"Thank you."

Sugarman arrived a few minutes early. The Ballard Studio was a pleasant and clean room, about the size of a small ballroom, with mirrors on three sides. Antonio greeted Sugarman cordially but asked if he would please have a seat for a few minutes.

"I be right with you," Antonio said.

While he was waiting, Sugarman kept looking at a large framed photograph that hung on one of the walls. It was of a dancing couple who seemed very serious and intense, and also very romantic.

After a few minutes Antonio walked up to Sugarman, holding the arm of a lovely, shapely lady in, perhaps, her forties or late thirties or early fifties. You couldn't tell her age from looking at her beautiful body. She was dressed in a casual but magnificent black skirt that flowed back and forth as she walked. Her low-cut blouse was lavender.

"Mr. Sugar, this is Margarita, who is going to be your dance partner."

"Buenos días," Margarita said as she shook hands with Sugarman.

"Wow. Yes. I hope so." Sugarman said. "Are you both Spanish?"

"No, no" Antonio said. "I am from Puerto Rico and

Margarita is from Colombia. But when you feel her in your arms and when you see how she moves, you will want to learn Spanish quickly."

They all laughed.

"So . . . the tango!" Antonio exclaimed. "Please face Margarita . . . yes, like that . . . but step in a little closer."

Sugarman moved closer and then gleefully put his arm around Margarita's waist, trying to look sexy as he jiggled his hips, waiting for Frank Sinatra to start singing.

"No, no, no," Antonio said with a little laugh. "We are not going to fox-trot, señor. Just face your beautiful partner, stand straight but not rigid . . . good . . . and now take a slow, deep breath."

Sugarman took a deep breath, wondering why on earth Laura Bailey sent him here.

"Now put your right arm around her back . . . higher up . . . raise your left hand, slowly, and offer it to your partner."

Sugarman did as he was told. Margarita cupped her hand into his. He looked like he was still at his high school prom, waiting for the band to start playing.

"Mr. Sugar, don't look *into* her eyes—even though they are very tantalizing. Just look a little bit off to one side of her face. You can still see her . . . you can feel her . . . but you *don't do* anything yet."

Sugarman put his hands on his hips in exasperation.

"But what am I waiting for? I mean, when is the dancing part?"

"When you are ready, señor."

"I'm ready! Where's the music?"

"Mr. Sugar, first you have to create your own music . . . even without the music," Antonio said with a smile.

"I think one of us is not dealing with a full deck here."

"The music gives you energy, yes, for sure. And that's good. But when the music is very fast, like, da da da da, you don't really have time to think. But in the silence—I mean the tango *without* the music—you start to feel the passion in your body. Then you dance. You understand?"

"Sure! You want me to look at her, but don't look at her. Be close, but not too close. Do some heavy breathing and wait till I feel the passion in my body—which I can tell you right now I felt as soon as she walked into the room—and then, when I'm ready, I start doing something, even if I don't know what I'm supposed to do."

"That's it," Antonio answered. "Perfect."

Sugarman took seven tango lessons, reluctantly, on Mondays and Thursdays at three o'clock. His partner was always Margarita.

Antonio was playing tango music now and Sugarman grasped little bits and pieces, here and there, of what Antonio was saying. But when he left the studio, he was always frustrated.

Each night as Sugarman tried to sleep, his brain kept hearing tango music. He kept visualizing where his feet were supposed to go and which one of Margarita's knees was bent. After the seventh lesson, he decided that enough was enough. He'd go back to the studio one more time, and then, after his eighth lesson, he would explain to Antonio that he had to go out of town on urgent business. "What do I owe you? Thank you very much," and that would be it.

But during the eighth lesson something extraordinary happened. He was facing Margarita in the usual way . . . he took a slow, deep breath, put his arm around her back, held up his hand for her to take, and, as he stood very still for a moment, he was suddenly overcome with passion. He began to dance.

Margarita followed, but Sugarman didn't think about the steps anymore—he began to improvise every movement and sudden pause. He felt the warmth of Margarita's body, and, at the same time, fleeting images of his wife sailed through his mind. He didn't know if the music had just started or was about to end . . . he just wanted to go on dancing.

When the music came to an end Margarita squeezed Sugarman's hand and kissed him on his cheek. He turned to Antonio, somewhat in a daze.

Antonio smiled. "Mr. Sugar," he said, "you begin to understand the tango a little bit. Congratulations."

That night, Sugarman picked up the phone and called the Chesterfield Hotel for Women. When he heard his wife's voice he said, "Hi, Georgia . . . how are you?"

"What is it you want, Charley?" she asked, not rudely, but as if she was expecting another request for her to wash his underwear and socks.

"I . . . just want to know how you're doing, honey. That's all. I worry about you sometimes, you know?"

"Do you, Charley."

"Yes, I do. More than you would ever imagine. Could I ask you a personal question, Georgia?"

After a long pause, Georgia said, "All right."

"Why did you marry me?"

"I don't want to talk about that."

"Please. I need a little help sometimes."

"Charley, I didn't know much about you when we were married. I just knew that you were a gentleman, that you were gentle, and I believed that you would always take care of me. I also used to love all the different colored shirts you wore from your haberdashery, when you came to pick me up and take me out to dinner. That's all."

"Did you love me?"

"I did then, yes."

"Could I ask you one more question, Georgia?"

"Charley—"

"Please, Georgia. It's very important to me. Just one more question."

"All right . . . if it won't take too long."

"I just want to know . . . if you'd like to go to the ballet with me sometime. Don Quixote is at the Met tonight . . . and Thursday night . . . if you want?"

There was a long pause.

"I'd like that very much, Charley."

The King of Hearts

I don't want to sound like an egomaniac, but I do know how to win at hearts. Perhaps I'm not an expert, but I think I'm pretty good, and I've had an awful lot of experience. But I'm telling you now that it can be dangerous. When I'm with Pauline, for instance, I usually get burned more times than I enjoy it. Sometimes, when I'm with Michele, I make out all right, and once or twice I've even been with both at the same time, but I've found that they are both brilliant at using the same technique that I'm going to teach you right now.

First of all, you've got to relax! Don't tense up when you make your first pass. If you only have three clubs or three diamonds—get rid of one or the other.

Secondly, if you're dealt a hand that has five or six spades, *including* the queen, pass three clubs or three diamonds—whichever would make you void in that suit—and then drop the queen of spades on someone else. Why should you get stuck with thirteen points, bam, just like that?

The last thing—at least for now—is this: If you're feeling really confident, well then, keep all of your high cards and pass three of your smallest. The whole point of this game is to avoid taking the queen of spades, or to take the queen and *all of the hearts*. If this works you will have shot the moon—which means that you don't get a single point while each of the other players gets stuck with twenty-six.

Good luck from your King of Hearts,

Robbie Sherman

Twelve people who barely knew each other formed a small club that we've named "Our Hearts." The only thing we had in common was that we all loved playing the game of hearts more than bridge. We meet every Friday evening at seven. Our little club is located in White Plains, New York, on the floor above our neighborhood ice cream parlor, Ciao Belly, close to where we all work and live.

Apart from my love of the game of hearts, I'm a feature writer for *Women's Health*, Westchester County's most popular magazine. I do a weekly column on health issues, but when our managing editor learned about Our Hearts—and also, I'm sure, because he heard that more and more people in Westchester County are playing hearts—he asked me to write an additional weekly feature giving our readers tips on how to win at hearts. My name is Robbie Sherman.

Pauline and Michele, the two women I referred to in my first column, are certainly the most cunning players in our little club.

Pauline is a somewhat cheerless woman, with straight dull brown hair and no flair at all for how to dress attractively. She is pretty enough, but not at all sexy. She's thin as a rail and cold as a cucumber. Michele, on the other hand, is a bona fide red-haired beauty and extremely sexy, especially in her multicolored skirts and her sweaters that emphasize her breasts. I don't know what Pauline or Michele do for a living—dental hygienists I would guess, because both of them are always pristine clean and their teeth are shiny white. They even carry a toothbrush with them on Friday nights so that they can brush their teeth right after our coffee and donut break.

Last Friday I decided to ask Michele—the sexy red-head—if she was free on Saturday night and if she'd like to go out with me for a movie and dinner. She was very gracious and even gave me a little hug, but said that she was busy Saturday.

My wife died two years ago and last Friday was the anniversary of our marriage, so I was a little lonely. After mulling it over for several minutes—while everyone was saying good night to each other—I asked the cheerless thin woman with dull brown hair to go out with me. This may sound silly, but I think there was something about Pauline's thinness that actually attracted me. I would have given you almost any odds that she'd turn me down, but I was wrong; she said yes immediately, with the slightest hint of a smile.

Daylight saving had begun, birds were chirping and flowers were beginning to bloom as I drove up to Pauline's house at a quarter to seven, which was plenty of time for us to see an early movie and then have dinner. I certainly didn't have anything else in mind.

I rang her doorbell and waited on the front porch. When she came out I was shocked, because this pale, dull-haired, drab dresser who wore straight, colorless skirts that never flared out at the bottom, was now wearing a beautiful lavender skirt that swished back and forth as she moved.

"You look lovely tonight, Pauline," I said as I gushed with surprise. *Is this is the same woman?* I asked myself. Even her dull hair had suddenly come alive.

"I didn't have to come straight from work tonight," she said, "the way I do on Fridays when I race to get to Our Hearts."

While I was driving we got into a little dispute. Pauline wanted to go to our local art house to see the re-release of Bette Davis in *Dark Victory*, and I was hoping to see the new Bond picture with Daniel Craig. Pauline is forty-one years old, divorced, and can sometimes be very brusque, whereas I'm forty-three, polite, and sometimes stubborn, but she's the girl and I'm the boy. My mother taught me to always walk on the curb side with a woman, always help her on with her coat, always open the door for her, and, if there's a conflict, always let her win.

In this case, the problem was quickly solved: We went to see *Dark Victory*.

The tears came streaming down Pauline's face when Bette Davis realized that she was going blind and that the end was imminent. Pauline took my hand and squeezed it, as if she were hoping against hope that there could still be a happy ending. But she and Bette both knew that was impossible.

I must say that I was also very moved, especially by Pauline taking my hand. I thought for sure that this simple human gesture would be something she would never do, or that she would think it was immature, but now I saw her through different eyes: the cold scientist, ruthless in hearts, suddenly revealing that she also had a human heart.

We went to Figaro—a small bistro nearby—and talked about the movie as we ate dinner.

"So, Pauline . . . what's your profession? I'll bet you dollars to donuts that you're a dental hygienist."

"I'm the chief of cardiothoracic and vascular surgery at Westchester Hospital Center," she said cheerfully as she chewed on her broccoli.

It felt like a full minute that my mouth was hanging open. To stop myself from looking like an oaf, I quickly stuffed a Brussels sprout into my mouth, but it got stuck in my throat and I couldn't get it up or down. I began coughing.

"Are you all right?" Pauline asked.

"Wen down . . . wong pipe," I tried to say as the coughing got worse. I think I was turning red.

Pauline yanked me out of my chair and stood behind my back.

"Raise your arms straight up," she ordered and then gave a hard tug just under my ribs. She tugged again, even harder, and out sailed the Brussels sprout like a little flying saucer.

"You're very naughty," she said. "You should eat slowly and chew your food before you swallow, like a big boy. Now sit down. Do you feel all right?"

"Yes. Thank you, Doctor."

When I took Pauline home she just said, "Thank you for the movie, Robbie, and the dinner, and for my not having to rush you to the emergency ward." She gave me a polite kiss on the cheek and said, "See you on Friday."

For our next lesson I want you to learn what you can do with a heart. You might think the best thing is to just get rid of it. But that can be treacherous, especially if you've got the 2, 3, 4, or 5 of hearts.

Ben, for example, is a member of our club who always sits on my right when I'm playing in a foursome. I don't think I'm paranoiac, but as soon as Ben sees me sit down, he runs to the table and sits next to me. Always on my right. Every time it's Ben's turn to pass cards to me, I know they're going to be his highest hearts. So here is today's lesson on how to avoid the trap: Always keep any small hearts that you've been dealt.

Good luck, from your King of Hearts,

Robbie Sherman

On our next Friday get-together, Pauline the doctor, was at another table and Michele, the sexy redhead, was on my left.

I thought I was imagining it at first, but it seemed that each time I passed three cards to Michele she would caress my hand very lightly as she took the cards. Friendly gesture? Perhaps, but after the third or fourth caress I think it was a signal.

After I lost that game and during our coffee and donut break, Michele wiggled up to me and said, "I'm free *this* Saturday, Robbie—if you still want to go to go out with me."

On Saturday night I picked Michele up at her home. She lived at 23 Very Merry Lane. When she told me her address I assumed it was a joke . . . but it wasn't.

"What do you feel like tonight, Michele?" I asked. "There's a new movie that came out this week that got great reviews."

"You mean *Rachel Getting Married*?" she asked.

"Yes, that's the one. Every paper is raving about it."

"I'm not in the mood for that one, Robbie. How about the new Bond picture? Feel like seeing 007 tonight . . . it's supposed to be very sexy?"

"Sure," I said.

After the opening action scene was over and the first female entered the scene, Michele took my hand and held on to it for the remainder of the movie. She squeezed my hand against her thigh during the very tense moments . . . and there were plenty of them. Michele was full of energy when the movie was over.

"What do you feel like eating tonight, Michele? There are lots of good restaurants just around the corner."

"You pick, Robbie. Someplace romantic."

My car was in a parking lot, so we walked a short way to Da Pietro, a small, candlelit Italian restaurant with very good country-style food and wines that weren't too expensive.

After our appetizer of melon with warm figs, we each sipped some Chianti while we waited for the main course.

"So, Michele . . . I want to know what you do for a living, but before you tell me, let me guess."

Michele smiled as her eyes glowed. "All right, guess!"

"I would say . . . that you are . . . a well-paid fashion model who works in New York City . . . at Saks Fifth Avenue or Bergdorf Goodman."

Michele laughed out loud and covered her mouth with her napkin.

"Did I hit it right on the nosie?" I asked.

"I'm afraid not, Robbie—I'm a dental hygienist. But thanks for the sweet compliment."

Michele held my hand as we walked to her front door. She took a key out of her purse, gave me a really seductive smile, put her arms around my neck, and pressed her lips on mine, moving them up and down and sideways for—let's say conservatively—two minutes. Then she said, "Good night dear, and thanks for the movie and dinner."

She opened her front door and threw me a kiss as she said: "Bye, Robbie. See you Friday."

On the following Friday night I was sitting next to Ben, who was on my right of course, and since both Pauline and Michele were at another table, I won the game easily.

I kept looking across the room, hoping to see if either Michele or Pauline was looking at me, but both were too concentrated on their game. All I wanted was a little smile from one of them and I would have smiled back and given a little wave. I felt as if I were in an old British movie—some silly comedy where a man falls in love with one girl and then realizes it's another girl he really loves, then changes his mind again and goes back to the first girl at the end of the movie. Silly, I know, but in those movies there was always a happy ending.

On Monday, my managing editor called me into his office.

"Robbie, I want a short profile as soon as possible on a gal who's now the chief of thoracic surgery at Westchester Hospital—a Doctor Pauline Faxon."

This should be fun, I thought. In the hospital the next morning, a receptionist pointed to a short, thin doctor in green scrubs and cap who was standing at the end of the hall, talking to a nurse. The receptionist said it was Pauline, but the doctor looked like a man to me.

I approached and hesitantly said, "Pauline?" It was her. She turned around and quickly took off her surgeon's cap when she saw it was me. Her hair was pinned up. "That's all, Liz" she said, to the nurse who was standing next to her. The nurse left immediately.

"I was expecting you today, Robbie, but you caught me a little off guard. I'm afraid I had an additional surgery this morning."

"Someone else get a Brussels sprout caught in his throat?"

"Oh, nothing that serious. This was just a quadruple bypass. Come," she said as she took my hand. "We'll go to my office. We can talk there and I badly need a cup of coffee."

After half an hour of questions about her training and how she had worked her way up to such a high position, I said, "Pauline, could I ask you one or two things that aren't about medicine . . . a few more personal questions, just to fill out the profile?"

"Go ahead. I can give you fifteen more minutes."

"You were married and divorced . . . is that right?"

"Yes," she said.

"Were you married very long? You don't have to answer that if you don't wish to."

"I don't mind. Nine years."

"Do you mind if I ask why you broke up with your husband just when you reached the top of your profession?"

"Because I reached the top of my profession," she said.

"Help me with that, please."

"My husband was an insurance salesman with two bosses above him. He didn't believe in a woman being the chief of anything. A doctor? Maybe. But chief of cardio-thoracic and vascular surgery? No! So he and his physical affection went out the window and he took up with women who were office clerks."

"I'm so sorry," I said.

"Don't be."

I looked up from my notes and stared at her for a few moments.

"Robbie—didn't you once say that your wife died two years ago?"

"Two and a half years ago. That's right."

"What was the cause of her death? I know she was very young."

"Heart attack."

After a short pause she said, "Well, I hope I gave you a good interview. Anything else? You look so pensive."

"Don't you get terribly lonely sometimes, Pauline?"

"I'm very happy with my work, Robbie. And if I find that I have a burning desire for attention and a little comfort . . . I play hearts," she said with a smile and then got up.

WHO GETS THE QUEEN?

Let's say that you've passed the queen of spades to Ben on your right and Pauline, who's on your left, just passed you the ace and king of spades. That's bad. BUT, you also have two smaller spades and you do know that Ben has the queen. So, when anyone starts leading spades and Ben plays a low one, you'll be safe playing the king or the ace. There are only thirteen spades in the deck, so by the time Ben is forced to play the queen, you'll only have a small spade left.

Good luck, from your King of Hearts,

Robbie Sherman

The telephone rang one evening.

"Robbie, it's Pauline Faxon. It's my birthday tomorrow night and I want to know if you'd go out to dinner with me."

"You mean just the two of us?"

"Yes. You were very kind to me during that interview and I'd like to recognize my birthday with someone I feel comfortable with. Whaddya say?"

"I'd be very happy to celebrate with you, Pauline."

We went to a beautiful French restaurant that Pauline knew. It was called Le Petit Bedon, which she said meant The Little Tummy. I was glad I had put on my best suit and most celebratory tie because tables of huge, gorgeous flowers greeted us as we walked in.

The lights were low and the food was delicious. We both had duck with cherries and a wine called Chambolle-Musigny. For dessert, the chef brought out a lovely lemon tart with one lit candle.

"From one chef to another chief," he said, and gave Pauline a kiss on each cheek. Then he and I and the waiters all sang "Happy Birthday." The restaurant was aptly named because, when we left, I did have a little tummy.

"Robbie, please come in and have a drink with me," Pauline said when we arrived at her home.

The home wasn't fancy, but the French provincial furniture and all the lamps in the living room had obviously been chosen with great care—simple and quietly tasteful.

Pauline came back into the living room where I was waiting. She was carrying a bottle of frosty Poire William brandy and two glasses.

After she poured our drinks, she said: "To us, Robbie—I think we both deserve a little happiness."

We clicked glasses and she leaned over and kissed me. Her kiss was not passionate but mine was. I put down both of our glasses and pulled her into my arms.

This extraordinarily thin surgeon with dull brown hair became more passionate than any woman I've ever known.

WINNING HEARTS

Dear readers:
Here's a little tip for you before I go on my two-week vacation. If you should fall behind by ten or even twenty points . . . you mustn't give up. Just concentrate and learn from the past; I promise that you can still win.

And here's a special message to those wonderful girls

who have proposed marriage to me, even though we've never met. Thank you for such a lovely compliment, but I've recently become engaged to a great heart surgeon. She's always cheerful and has the loveliest brown hair.

Good luck to you all from your King of Hearts,

Robbie Sherman

The Kiss

Becky Goodenough fell hopelessly in love with Robert, a penniless young man who wrote beautiful poems and two novels but couldn't sell one page of his work for enough money to buy a cup of hot chocolate in the cold Milwaukee winter of 1947.

Becky and Robert met each other at the Milwaukee Community Theatre, where casting was open to anyone in the city. They both auditioned and were cast in the leading roles in *Romeo and Juliet*.

Becky was an obvious choice . . . a lovely girl, seventeen years old, with a face that had the clear, creamy skin of a baby, and with her long, golden brown hair she looked perfect for the part.

Robert was twenty-four years old and wasn't what you would traditionally call handsome, but he had a unique voice and a striking presence on stage. The director also thought that Robert was a natural actor, even though he looked like a starving Romeo.

Becky and Robert fell in love, on stage and in real life, during the third day of rehearsals, when they kissed during the balcony scene.

All the actors worked solely for the love of art and the desire to show off. To survive, Robert had a job delivering the *Milwaukee Journal* between 5:30 and 6:30 each morning, for which he was paid eighteen dollars a week. After he finished his paper route, he spent the whole day writing; then he ate a tuna salad sandwich on his way to rehearsals, which began each weekday at 7:00 p.m.

One evening after rehearsal, Becky asked Robert why they couldn't go to his house and touch each other and see each other's naked bodies.

"Don't you want to?" Becky asked.

"Of course I do," Robert said, "but you're too young, and I wouldn't feel right about it."

"Oh, pooh!" was Becky's reply.

Becky's father was named Boris Goodenough, aptly named after Mussorgsky's opera, *Boris Godunov*—the story of a Russian tyrant who became tsar—but the last name was slightly altered when his family came through immigration. An officer changed Godunov to Goodenough, believing it would be easier for Americans to pronounce. The change didn't bother Boris's father because he couldn't hear the difference.

When Boris was twenty-eight, he married a beautiful, frail woman named Sarah, who had also come from Russia. The two lovers were giddy when they talked about how many children they would have, but Sarah died giving birth to their only child, Becky.

When Boris heard that his beautiful seventeen-year-old daughter had fallen in love with a twenty-four-year-old "beggar who doesn't have a pot to pee in" he shouted, "YOU ARE NOT PERMITTED TO LOVE! You're too young and that's it and that's all!"

At Becky's urging, Robert, the penniless boyfriend, came to meet Boris Goodenough. Becky had hopes that a little ice might melt if only her father could see what a beautiful young man Robert was.

"Daddy, this is the gentleman I've told you about," she said with glowing cheeks. "This is Robert. He has a master's degree in English literature from Marquette University."

"I'm very pleased to meet you, Mr. Goodenough," Robert said nervously as he extended his arm for a handshake.

"Do you have a last name," Boris Goodenough asked, "or are you too poor?"

"Frost, sir."

"Robert Frost?" Mr. Goodenough repeated skeptically.

"Yes, sir. Our family name was Frost. My father chose Robert for my first name because of the poet Robert Frost, whom he admired."

"WHOM he admired! Oh, well—that's different. We've got a 'whom' in the house."

Becky tried to cut off her father's sarcasm, but Boris shouted, "Shaaa!"

"May I ask what your father's name is, Mr. Frost?"

"Jack, sir," Robert replied.

". . . Jack Frost?"

"Yes, sir."

"And your mother?"

"Early."

". . . Your mother's name is Early?"

"Well . . . it was actually Early May, but all of her friends just call her Early," Robert replied.

"Of course . . . that's only natural. And where are Jack and Early Frost right now?"

"They're in Brazil, sir. They left when my father was offered a job there. I live alone now."

"May I ask what you do for a living, Mr. Robert Frost?"

"I'm an artist, sir."

"You mean you paint pictures?"

"No, sir, I mean . . . well, I don't know how wonderful my poems or novels are . . . I just mean that, to me, being an artist is a way of satisfying the need you feel to create something beautiful."

"I see," Boris replied. "How much does a good 'need' pay a fellow these days?"

"Daddy!" Becky shouted, getting more and more upset with the conversation.

"What? I'm asking an intelligent question," Boris replied innocently. "Maybe not an *artistic* question, but a father's question. Wouldn't you agree, Robert, son of Jack and Early May Frost?"

"Yes, sir, I would. I understand and agree with you completely," Robert said after seeing the panic on Becky's face.

"And the answer to your question is . . . that it doesn't pay anything, Mr. Goodenough . . . except for the love I feel that floods my heart every time I write."

"Well . . . that counts for something," Boris said. "Not enough for a steak dinner, or a chicken, or a hamburger, or a peanut butter sandwich . . . or a pickle . . . but as long as it keeps flooding you, that's the important thing. However . . . YOU ARE NOT PERMITTED TO LOVE MY DAUGHTER, and that's it and that's all."

Robert left the house brokenhearted. Becky cried. Boris went back to reading his book: *How to Play Chess and WIN*.

One month later, after *Romeo and Juliet* had finished its three-week run, Becky was cast as Marguerite Gautier in the Milwaukee Community Theatre production of *The Lady of the Camellias*, by Alexandre Dumas . . . the same part that Greta Garbo played in the movie *Camille*.

This time—also on the third day of rehearsals—Becky fell hopelessly in love with the tall and extremely handsome young man, Gerhardt Schlegel, who was playing the part of Armand, the wealthy aristocrat, played by Robert Taylor in the movie. When the production finished its three-week run, Becky ran off with Gerhardt to Chicago, sending her father a short letter:

Dear Daddy,

I'm in love. Really, truly in love this time. And I'm safe, so don't worry about me. Gerhardt Schlegel is a wonderful young man and it's time I grew up. We're going to live in Chicago for a while, but I'll write soon.

Love,
Becky

She also wrote a note to Robert.

Dear Robert,

I'm desperately in love with a wonderful young man who is closer to my own age. You and I had nowhere to go, so I'm afraid it's over. I know you wish me happiness.

Becky

Robert was devastated by the news. He wandered the streets of Milwaukee. He was in a daze as he passed the hardware store on Burleigh Street where he used to buy his pencils, and the Sherman movie theater where he used to go with his parents when he was a little boy, and Guten's delicatessen on Center Street, where he now looked through the window and saw chickens turning on a spit, which made his stomach cry in pain. He looked at the menu posted outside, just to see what he *might* order if he had the money to pay for it.

After hours of wandering the neighborhood, his gloveless hands were so cold that he couldn't feel them anymore, even though he kept them in his pockets.

Just when he thought he might freeze to death, he looked up and found, to his great surprise, that he was standing in front of Boris Goodenough's front door. It was seven o'clock in the evening and the sun had vanished hours ago.

At this point, Robert was beyond fear. Since he saw that the lights were on in both the living room and the kitchen, he rang the doorbell. He kept ringing it—even leaning on it—until the door finally opened. And there was Boris, unshaven and looking like a faded gray portrait of misery. Boris didn't say "Hello" or "Get the hell out of here"; he just moaned "oy" four times and finally said, "You want some tea?"

The two mourners commiserated over tea and strudel for two hours. Boris kept pushing food at Robert. Every time Robert started to say, "Thank you, but I really—" Boris would say, "Shaaa! Just eat! It'll do you good."

After half an hour together they stopped talking about Becky. Instead, they talked about chess, after Boris learned that Robert had played chess on his college team.

After six helpings of tea in a glass, the Russian way, plus ten pieces of strudel that were forced upon him, happily, Robert stood at the front door, ready to say good night, when Boris suddenly threw his arms around Robert and hugged him, holding on to him for ten or fifteen seconds. Boris finally said, "Get out of here and don't catch cold!"

Robert and Boris played chess and ate dinner together for the next ten nights. The food was delivered from Guten's delicatessen, where Boris had a charge account.

On the first night they played, Boris looked at the chessboard, with its beautiful porcelain chess pieces all set up.

"White or black?" he asked, as if any answer Robert gave would be a trick.

"Oh, it doesn't matter to me, sir. You choose," Robert answered.

"I'm asking *you*—white or black?"

"White," Robert answered.

Boris turned the chessboard around so that the white pieces were facing Robert, but somehow he suspected that a trick had already been played on him.

Since Robert was playing white, he had the first move and quickly pushed one of his pawns to a spot that would be easy for Boris to take. Boris yelled: "AHA! Queen's Gambit! I knew you'd do that—you not-so-clever sucker. All right, how do you like *this?*" he said, taking Robert's white pawn with bravado.

Robert was prepared and quickly moved another pawn.

Boris looked puzzled. "What the hell kind of a cockamamie move is that?" Boris asked.

"The Sicilian Defense," Robert answered.

"WE'RE NOT IN SICILY!" Boris shouted. "Why do you do what a mafioso would do?"

"Because I let you have more control of the center, while I build a safe wall of pawns," Robert answered.

"Hmmn!" Boris groaned.

The game lasted another seven minutes, after which Robert quietly and politely said, "Checkmate."

Boris stared at him for several seconds, then quickly got up, saying, "I'm hungry! Let's have something to eat before we start another game. And this time I won't feel sorry for a poor artist—I'll play for real."

Over the next seven days Robert won seven games. On the eighth day of this little marriage, Boris finally won a game and crowed like a rooster. "ALL RIGHT—NOW WE'RE TALKING BUSINESS! Come on, let's eat! I'm starved."

When they finished their brisket of beef with red beets and mashed potatoes, Boris poured both of them a glass of tea and put a plate of eight or nine pieces of strudel on the table.

"By the way, I want to read one of those stories you've written that floods your heart," Boris said affectionately.

The next day, Robert brought Boris one of his short novels. He also let Boris win the chess game that night, just to put him in a receptive mood.

Boris was completely puzzled over the title . . . *The Last of the Running Footmen.*

"What the hell is a running footman?" Boris asked.

"Well, we don't have them in Milwaukee," Robert said with a little laugh, as he took a sip of tea.

"So answer me—what is a running footman?" Boris asked again.

Robert began slowly. "In the eighteenth century, wealthy people in England always had a young man who would help his master and mistress in and out of their carriage, and then he ran alongside the horses until the carriage reached its destination."

"They had slavery?"

"No, they had money."

"And that's all they did? . . . help them into a carriage?"

"No, they always had a pole that they carried with them on rainy days, just in case the carriage got stuck in the mud. Then the running footman would have to help the carriage driver get the carriage out of the mud. He also had to run ahead and advise the nearest innkeeper that aristocrats or royalty were coming . . . it was sort of like making a reservation at a restaurant . . . then run back as fast as he could to help his master and mistress out of the carriage and down the little carriage stair until their feet were safely planted on the ground."

"How much did these fellows get paid?"

"I don't know, Mr. Goodenough—I don't know what a pound was worth then—but it wouldn't have been very much."

"Well, since you're not my running footman, you can now call me Boris."

On the tenth night, they sat at the card table where the chessboard was already set up, but before they began playing, Mr. Goodenough stared at Robert for almost half a minute.

"Is something wrong, Boris?" Robert asked.

"I read your book."

"Oh . . ." Robert said softly, expecting the worst.

"I thought it was going to be all about helping this wealthy lady in and out of a carriage," Boris said. "But instead, I find out that this schlimazel footman falls in love with her, and she encourages him, and then she drops him like a hot potato and runs away with a baron or a count or some other schlemiel. Sound familiar?" Boris asked.

Robert gave a sigh. "Yes, I think I understand what you're getting at."

"Robert Frost—the only thing you understand is heartache and pathos and love."

"What else is there?" Robert answered.

"Food, money, and marriage with a beautiful woman who dies giving birth to a beautiful baby girl, who grows up and breaks your heart. Nice things like that."

As if on cue, the front door opened and Becky walked in. When she saw the two men sitting together she froze like a statue.

"So, what brings you back?" Boris asked without emotion.

"It's my birthday," Becky answered plaintively.

Robert looked at her, but couldn't speak.

"By the way . . . how old are you now?" Boris asked. "Forty-five . . . fifty . . . ?"

"I'm eighteen, Daddy," Becky mumbled.

"And how is Count Gerhardt Gehagenmachenschlagen these days? Is he waiting in his carriage?"

"No," Becky replied softly.

"DID YOU OR DIDN'T YOU?" Boris burst out. "That's all I want to know."

"I DID! But it wasn't anything like what I thought it would be," she said as tears welled up in her eyes. "And Gerhardt kept saying, 'Don't worry, Becky, its normal. We just have to keep trying. It will get much better, you'll see.' But it didn't get better—it got worse!"

Now rain poured from her eyes.

"I hated all the hair on his chest and the way he smelled."

"THEN WHAT THE HELL DID YOU RUN AWAY WITH HIM FOR?" Boris asked.

"BECAUSE I THOUGHT HE WOULD BE SWEET AND GENTLE AND CONSIDERATE—THE WAY ROBERT IS. BUT HE WAS A FILTHY ROTTEN PIG!" she screamed as she ran up the stairs to her bedroom.

Silence.

The two men sat motionless, each in his own thoughts.

Finally: "White or black?" Boris asked.

The two men played chess for fifteen minutes without talking; then Becky came down the stairs and stood in front of them.

"Oh? More good news?" Boris asked.

Becky stared at her father defiantly.

"Yes! In case you didn't know it, your beautiful, angelic daughter is a spoiled, rotten brat!"

After this news bulletin, Becky turned away quietly and walked back up the stairs with as much dignity as she could manage.

By late March, the earth showed the earliest signs of flowers that seemed to be yawning, as if they were trying to decide if it was time to get up.

The Community Theatre held auditions for their next production, *Much Ado About Nothing*. Becky and Robert auditioned and won the leading roles.

By mid-April, daffodils burst open all along the soft green grass on both sides of Sherman Boulevard, showing their beautiful but fragile yellow faces.

ONE YEAR LATER

Boris Goodenough sat alone at the wedding table with only half a heart because his wife wasn't there to squeeze his hand at the sight of Becky in her beautiful silk and chiffon wedding gown. He was also a little sad because the gown cost ninety dollars and the ballroom at the Schroeder Hotel cost a hundred and twenty dollars, which, for Milwaukee in 1948, was a considerable amount of money.

He watched Becky feed a huge slice of wedding cake into the mouth of Robert Frost, his son-in-law of five minutes.

As the bride and groom kissed, both their chins got painted white with frosting. All the guests laughed. The small band—which cost three hundred and fifty dollars for the evening—began to play Cole Porter's "So In Love." Robert waved to Boris and Becky threw a kiss to her father as she and Robert Frost walked to the dance floor. While they danced, Becky ate Robert's chin.

Boris was now forty-eight years old and was feeling terribly lonely, although he would never admit such a thing to anyone, because it might be taken as a sign of weakness.

Most of the wedding guests were friends of the bride and groom. Boris invited the few friends he had, but— truth to tell—he wasn't a very popular or gregarious man. Of course people patted him on the back and belched out, "Congratulations Boris," but no one wanted to actually sit down and talk with him; they only spoke as they passed him on their way to the bar or the buffet table, where they drank schnapps or beer and ate chopped liver sandwiches and strudel. The charge for food and drink was three dollars and fifty cents per guest.

His new son-in-law, Robert Frost, was not, strictly speaking, an Orthodox Jew, but Boris forgave him for that, eventually. Robert had fought in the war against Hitler and was wounded liberating the town of Rennes, France, and Boris respected him for that. Robert Frost converted to Judaism when he knew he wanted to marry Becky.

As Boris sipped a glass of Blatz beer, lost in memories of his own wedding as he imagined how gracefully he used to glide and twirl his beautiful wife across the floor and how nervous she was at their first kiss that night, an attractive woman walked up silently and sat down beside him.

The woman was in her early forties. She had a soft face and penetrating light blue eyes that had seen both suffering and joy. Her brown and red hair was shot through with streaks of gray. She didn't wear makeup except for the faintest glow of rose on her lips. The woman just sat and watched Boris, without moving or making a sound. When he finally became aware of her presence, he turned and looked at her.

"My name is Olivia Weldon," she said in a soft voice. "I want to congratulate you on this lovely occasion."

Boris stared her, silently questioning the audacity of this intruder who interrupted his dancing. He answered in his usual offhanded manner.

"Thank you," he said, and quickly turned away.

Olivia Weldon punched him playfully in the shoulder.

"You can't get off that easily, Mr. Bad Enough," she said with a beatific smile. "I've heard about your crude manner and I'm not put off by it. I can see that your heart is filled with love, and also lots of pain tonight."

Boris let out an "oy!" and then said, "Are you one of these cockamamie psychics who came here to make money off my guests by telling fortunes? You're wasting your time if you think—"

Olivia took Boris's hand and held it gently. "I really just wanted to meet you, Boris."

"Why?"

"Because I found you very attractive," she said.

"What the hell do you mean, 'found' me? . . . You mean, you 'find' me attractive? If you do, you're a meshugana. I'm a big hulk who's twenty-five pounds overweight and balding and who isn't interested in women anymore, so pick on some other schlemiel."

"No. I mean I 'found' you attractive, Boris . . . after I read one of your poems."

"I only wrote one poem in my life and you couldn't possibly have read it," Boris shouted.

"But I did," Olivia answered quietly.

"Oh, yes? What's the name of my beautiful poem?"

" 'Saying Goodbye,' " she answered.

Boris' face froze with his mouth half open. He kept staring at Olivia Weldon as if she might be a figment of his imagination.

"When I said I found you attractive, Boris, I meant your heart. Although I also think you're still a handsome man, despite your gruff manner and those twenty-five pounds, which is why you always wear an overcoat."

"What the hell are you talking about, 'always wear an overcoat?' I only go out maybe twice a week," Boris proclaimed with a vengeance.

"I think you also wear it inside your house," Olivia rebutted softly.

"AND WHY WOULD I WEAR AN OVERCOAT INSIDE MY OWN HOUSE, MADAM FREUD?"

"To hide your nakedness," Olivia answered sweetly.

"What's your name again?" Boris asked after a frustrated pause.

"Olivia. But some people call me sweetheart."

"Okay, sweetheart—I gave that poem to my almost son-in-law over seven months ago, after he showed me a story he had written. Why in God's name would he give it to you?"

"I was his teacher," Olivia answered.

"Teacher of what—meshuganism?"

"No, I'm a teacher of American literature and poetry. I teach a night class at Marquette University."

There was a long pause while Boris pondered his next move.

"Listen to me—sweetheart—I'm not a poet. I don't want to be a poet. So why in the world would Robert give you some sentimental, schlocky poem I gave him?"

"Your poem isn't sentimental, Boris. Sentimental just means unearned emotion, and your emotion was certainly earned, because your heart was bleeding after your wife died. And it isn't schlocky, either—if there is such a word—it's actually quite beautiful."

Two tears managed to sneak out of Boris's eyes without permission, but he quickly slapped them away.

"One night in class we were talking about free verse," Olivia said quickly, to cover his embarrassment, "and Robert thought your poem was a perfect example."

"What the hell does 'free verse' mean—that you don't pay for it?" Boris asked.

"Sort of," Olivia responded. "It's a little like playing tennis without a net."

"JEWS DON'T PLAY TENNIS!" Boris declared, resorting to his roaring mode again.

"Well, *you* did in your poem, Boris. You wrote without worrying about the rules—just spoke from your heart."

Boris stared at his adversary. *Knight to queen's pawn*, he thought, and then spoke carefully with his idea of a sweet voice.

"How do you know so much about bleeding hearts—if you don't mind my asking? Have you ever been married, sweetheart?"

Now it was Olivia who sat silently. Her eyes stared at the folds in her light blue and lavender dress for half a minute. Then she looked up at Boris.

"I was about to be married for life, several years ago," she answered.

"Who was the lucky guy?" Boris asked with a smirk.

"Jesus."

Now Boris was on shaky ground and he knew it. He decided to play it carefully. "What was the fellow's last name?"

"Christ."

"Is this a joke?"

"No, Boris. No joke. I was a nun who changed her mind."

"When was this?" Boris asked almost politely.

"Fifteen years ago."

"What, did you get into a fight or something?" Boris asked.

"Not with Jesus," she said with a little laugh. "It was with someone else. I was sent to live in Newark, New Jersey, to help the homeless and hungry. I loved what I was doing and I worked my ass off—oh, don't looked so shocked, Boris— but my mother superior's way of helping people was archaic. I knew I could do much more good if I had a little freedom to use my brain. But she never asked me to do something—she demanded that I do it. After seven years— shortly before taking my final vows—I rebelled from her insistence on idiotic obedience and I left."

Boris' demeanor softened considerably. "You couldn't have been very old," he said.

"I was twenty-six and still a virgin," she said with a smile.

"Oy," Boris sighed. "Now I'm going to listen to a nun telling me about her sex life."

"You don't have to. But it might do you some good. Most of my experiences were with Jewish men."

"Why would a nice Catholic woman like you—who also happened to be a nun for a while—ever want to go out with a Jew?"

"Because I'm Jewish," Olivia said.

"Oy gevalt! Now what the hell is that supposed to mean, if you'll pardon my language, sweetheart?"

"My mother was Jewish and my father was Catholic."

"Are you making a joke?" Boris asked, suspecting a trap.

"No. If your mother is Jewish, you're Jewish. You know that."

As Boris wiped the perspiration from his forehead, Becky rushed up breathlessly and threw her arms around him.

"I'm going to our room upstairs to change into my honeymoon outfit, Daddy. And then we're going to sneak out quietly. I just wanted to say good-bye and to tell you how happy I am . . . and that I love you."

Becky ran off. Robert Frost, who was surrounded by his friends, waved from the dance floor, touched his lips, and threw Boris an imaginary kiss.

Boris got up, waved back, and then sat down again, not quite sure anymore of what to do with his life. Olivia sat beside him and held his hand.

"What's happening all of a sudden?" Boris asked as he looked at Olivia. "I don't even know why you're here . . . and don't tell me you're an angel or something like that. I don't want to hear that kind of stuff."

"I'm not an angel, Boris. I promise you."

"What's your name again?"

"Olivia."

"That's right. I remember. Your friends call you sweetheart."

"Yes."

"By any chance . . . do you play chess?"

"No, I don't. I'm sorry."

"That's all right. I'll teach you."

"How about a kiss, Boris?"

Boris stared into Olivia's beautiful light blue eyes, then

slowly and gently lifted her out of her chair and kissed her. They shared a very long kiss as passion began to stir in Boris's body once again. When they finally parted, Olivia said, "Would you like to dance?"

"I don't remember how, sweetheart."

"That's all right. I'll teach you."

Olivia took Boris's hand and led him onto the dance floor as the band played "It Had to Be You."

The Hollywood Producer

Sonny and Buddy were having dinner at the newest and most chic singles club in Los Angeles, one of those high-tech places that are so packed every night that you have to make a reservation three to four weeks in advance and then you usually find out that it had to close after one year.

"What're you staring at, Buddy?"

"See that honey over there?" Buddy asked.

"Where?"

"Sitting on that bar stool. The cute one with the fake blond hair."

"So . . . ?" Sonny asked after spotting her. "You wanna make a play for her?"

"No, she wouldn't give me the time of day."

"Don't be so sure. You can't always be right *all* the time, Buddy. How about if I invite her over to have a drink with us?"

"No, she'll take one look at me and laugh," Buddy said. "And then she'll say she's waiting for her boyfriend, who happens to be a little late tonight."

"How the hell do you know all this?" Sonny asked.

"Guess!" Buddy said as he took a sip of his Absolut.

"I know what's wrong with you, Buddy."

"Oh yeah, Dr. Einstein—what's wrong with me?"

"You've got a female inferiority complex about girls."

"Yeah, that's right! You should open an office and hang up a shingle."

"All right, smart aleck—supposing you're wrong this time. At least let me ask her—what've you got to lose?"

"My dignity, my self-respect, my night's sleep, my confidence with business deals . . . and my appetite for the steak I just ordered."

Sonny took a long sip of his Brandy Alexander, trying to figure out the best psychological approach for handling Buddy.

"Okay," Sonny said. "I think you're all wet and I'm willing to pay for your dinner tonight if I'm wrong. Is that a deal?"

"It's your nickel, start talking," Buddy answered, using one of his favorite lines from a movie he saw when he was nine years old.

Sonny walked over to the peroxide blond while Buddy watched. After a few seconds, the blond lady turned to look at Buddy, smiled sweetly, and waved. After she and Sonny talked for a few more seconds, Sonny came back, sat down, and took a slow sip of his drink.

"So?" Buddy asked. "Got any great news to share with your pal?"

Sonny hesitated and finally said, "You win."

"Oh, really? What a shock! What'd she say?"

"Well . . . she said she'd love to any other time . . . she

really did . . . but she's waiting for her boyfriend, who happens to be a little late tonight."

"Gosh, what a surprise," Buddy said.

Sonny put his drink down.

"You're my best friend, Buddy. How come I can't see what's wrong with you?"

" 'Cause you're not a girl," Buddy answered.

"Apart from that—and the fact that you're nuts—what else is so wrong with you that I can't see it?" Sonny asked.

"I'm short, I'm overweight for a little squirt, I still have leftover eczema scars on my otherwise beautiful soft face—and I'm losing my hair in the front."

Sonny sat quietly for half a minute.

"Well, I'll tell ya something, Buddy. You can't grow taller and you can't change your hair genes, BUT—you *can* get some platform shoes and start losing weight instead of eating steak and French fries. And you *can* join a health club and exercise with a trainer and get yourself in shape instead of sitting here talking about why girls don't go for you."

"I plan on doing all that stuff, and more," Buddy said. "This was going to be my last night to binge until you spoiled it by playing Dr. Freud."

"Are you lying to me?" Sonny asked.

"I don't lie . . . except to myself sometimes."

"Well, tell me—what're you going to do that's even more than what I said you should do?" Sonny asked.

"Hair transplants."

"What the hell are you talking about?" Sonny asked.

"HAIR! I'm talking about HAIR, Sonny. You go to the doctor's office, they give you some injections, they take out some hair from the back of your head—where I've got bushels—and they plant it in the front of your head. It's like gardening."

"Does it work?"

"You think I'd do it otherwise?"

"Does it hurt?"

"Not much. They make you go bye-bye for a little while, wrap up your head and send you home. Then you wait for three months and, bingo—hair starts popping up like string beans."

"You know I love you, Buddy—but may I make a tiny suggestion?" Sonny asked.

"Be my guest."

"Do the hair thing if you want to, but do it *last*! When a cute girl is sitting at the bar and looks at you, do you think she says, 'Oh, too bad he doesn't have enough hair in the front of his head.' No! She says, 'Look at that fatty boom boom over there. If he lost twenty or thirty pounds, he'd be kinda cute.'"

"I told you I'm *gonna* do *all* that stuff, Sonny. But I want to do the hair thing first."

"Why?" Sonny asked.

"Because when I look in the mirror, I don't see the fat around my stomach, I don't see how tall or short I am, I just see my forehead growing higher and higher. Do you get it?"

"Buddy, I can't wait till three months from now when Clark Gable suddenly appears."

One month later, the swelling in Buddy's head had disappeared and he looked fine again, except that his weight had gone up instead of down. When he and Sonny were having lunch at Junior's delicatessen and Buddy ordered pastrami on rye with coleslaw and Russian dressing, Sonny shook his head in disbelief.

"May I ask why you're ordering the most fattening thing on the menu except for my corned beef sandwich?"

"Business is bad, Sonny. I think I'm gonna have to get out of orange groves and go into show business."

"Have you gone south of the border? Since when did you learn how to act?"

"Not acting, schmuck—producing! You don't have to know that much to be a producer, you just have to find a good script and sell it. And I know movies as good as anyone—even better than most producers."

"What about the health club and losing all the weight and transforming your body into Clark Gable's?"

"Sonny, can you pat your head and rub your tummy at the same time?"

"What the hell has rubbing my tummy got to do with being a producer?"

"Because I can't work out and lose weight and run around a track a dozen times until I know I've got some business where I can make a killing."

"Why do you have to make a killing? Why can't you just make enough money to enjoy yourself and live happily ever after, like Snow White?"

"Because that's how you keep score."

"WHO'S KEEPING SCORE?" Sonny asked, getting fired up.

"THEY are! Everyone I know."

The waiter came with their sandwiches and cream sodas and Sonny sat there, watching Buddy. He remembered sitting beside Buddy's bed in the hospital when Buddy had his bypass operation, and the medical smells and the nurses who kept coming in to check Buddy's temperature and blood pressure. Sonny decided he'd better not get him too excited.

"So, have you read any good scripts lately?" Sonny asked as he picked up his sandwich and took a bite.

"One or two possibilities. But I need to work with the authors a little bit . . . get them on the right track," Buddy answered.

"Good. Good." Sonny said.

Spring had sprung, and so had Buddy's transplants. His forehead was now full with thick brown, curly hair, but his pants were too tight and had to be let out an inch around the waist.

One evening, when Sonny was out of town visiting his daughter in Milwaukee, Buddy decided to go to that restaurant where he had seen the peroxide blond, not expecting to find her, of course, but maybe some other cutie to test out his new appearance.

The restaurant was full but not packed the way it used to be, and the crowd seemed a little different now, more dressed up and slightly older.

Buddy sat at one of the small tables for two. It faced the bar and he could watch the people and the food pass back and forth in front of him as he sipped his Absolut.

One woman in particular caught his eye: a very attractive redhead sitting alone at the bar. Her red hair was streaked ever so lightly with a hint of blond, and her face—if not what Buddy would call "a real looker"—was very attractive. There was also something exotic about her looks and the way she dressed.

He couldn't tell if the woman was waiting for someone, but Buddy assumed—as good looking as she was—that she wouldn't come to this beautiful restaurant alone. Still, he could test out his Clark Gable hair and platform shoes, and at least he wouldn't be much shorter than she. *What've you got to lose?* he said to himself, and walked over to her. Willie Nelson's romantic standards were floating softly through the speakers.

"How ya doin'? I'm Mark Silberman, the Hollywood producer—remember me? Didn't you read for me and my director a couple weeks ago?"

The redhead looked at him, flattered by what he said but a little confused.

"I'm sorry, Mr. Silberman. I'm afraid I don't remember," she said with a smile. "I wish it *had* been me."

"Oh, no—please—I'm the one who's sorry! I didn't mean to disturb you; it's just that—with your face and body, you'd be a knockout on film."

"You're very kind Mr. Silberman. Thank you."

"No, I'm not kind—I just always tell the truth. Anyway, sorry again for disturbing you."

Buddy started to walk away and then stopped—as if he had just thought of something.

"By the way, are you alone? I mean—would you like to have a drink with me? I'm sitting right over there, at that little table across the way."

The redhead looked at Buddy's eyes, as if she were not quite sure how to respond.

"Well . . . I *was* waiting for someone, but it seems I've been stood up," she said holding back the hint of a tear.

"Well, the hell with that schmuck," Buddy said with growing confidence. "Why don't you let me buy you a drink?"

"You're very kind, Mr. Silberman. Thank you. That would be nice," she said.

She started to pick up the remains of her frozen daiquiri when Buddy said, "Forget that honey—we'll get you a new one."

They walked over to Buddy's table just as the music changed to Harry Nilsson singing "What'll I do?" With

Buddy's platform shoes, the redhead was only about an inch taller than he was. Buddy helped her into a chair.

"What can I get for you, honey? A drink, a shrimp cocktail, a steak, a lobster? WAIT! First of all, what's your name? I can't go on calling you 'honey.'"

"Charlotte. Charlotte Butler," she answered.

"Great name! What'll you have, Charlotte?"

"Another frozen daiquiri would be wonderful. Thank you, Mr. Silberman."

"Oh, please—now that we're pals, just call me Buddy. That's what half the world calls me."

"How sweet. I love that for a name," Charlotte said.

Buddy waved as a waiter walked by.

"A frozen daiquiri for the young lady and another Absolut for me, please."

Buddy turned to Charlotte. "Now then—tell me about yourself. NO! I take that back. That's what all producers say and I hate it and I don't wanna be like them. May I ask how long you've been living in L.A?"

"I came here four years ago and—"

"From where?" Buddy interrupted.

"A small town in Iowa," she answered. "You wouldn't have heard of it."

"Test me!" Buddy said.

"Keokuk," she answered with a little smile.

"Two movie theaters, one so-so restaurant, no bars, and a helluva lot a corn."

Charlotte put her face into her napkin to cover her laugh.

"Right on, Buddy. That's why I left," she finally said. "How in the world could you know Keokuk, Iowa?"

"Oh, I used to work that town when I was in a whole other business. The Bible Belt! Right, Charlotte?"

"You're telling me," she said. "That's why I left."

Charlotte smiled at him softly as she looked at his eyes.

"You're awfully nice, Buddy. You're not married, are you?"

"Not on your life," Buddy answered. "I mean—not yet."

"Do you have a steady?" Charlotte asked.

"Naw, nothing that I would call 'steady.' Not yet, anyway. But who knows?—I could get lucky," he said, looking at Charlotte in as romantic a way as he knew how.

When their drinks arrived, Buddy raised his glass and said, "Here's lookin' at you, kid."

"Here's to you, Buddy dear."

Buddy was as happy as he had been for months.

Charlotte reached under the table, placed a hand on Buddy's thigh, and gave it a gentle squeeze.

"Buddy . . . have you ever had sex with a transvestite before?"

Passion

I've always thought of passion as an uncontrollable desire—I mean a feeling that so clouds your mind that it makes you forget where you are and even who you are. Anyway, that's what I thought when I was thirteen year old and that's what I always thought I wanted, but I've never experienced it except in my imagination.

My name is Max Baer and I have a small but very good business in Darien, Connecticut, called Chauffeurs Unlimited—We Drive Your Car. Our rates are almost half the price of the big limo companies and I drive most of the clients myself, although I have two men who help me out if things get very busy. Most people want to go to the theater or the airport, but some women just want to go shopping in the ritziest places in New York.

On a sunny day in April, when the ice and snow had finally disappeared and the daffodils and tulips were starting to show signs of life, I was asked to pick up a woman at 2:00 p.m. from a house on East Hunting Ridge Lane, in Stamford, which was close to where I lived. With that address I was hoping the lady wouldn't be another ritzy-ditsy snob.

The house turned out to be a beautiful old-world

farmhouse, nineteenth century I would guess, made of stone and wood. An Oldsmobile was waiting in the driveway. I parked my Chevy, straightened my tie—I always wear a suit and tie when I'm driving clients—and rang the doorbell.

The door opened and I was confronted by a stout, gray-haired lady who looked as strong as an ox. Her arm was wrapped around a small young woman—perhaps twenty-three or -four—who had a stupid expression that seemed like it was frozen onto her face because it didn't move or change. She was wearing a red beret that covered half of her beautiful red hair, and she wore an overcoat that was way too big for her. I'm sure it was a man's coat.

The stout lady gave me the key to the Oldsmobile and gave the young woman a kiss on the cheek, mumbling something in a foreign language, and then turned to me.

"You take good care of my girl, yes?" she ordered.

"I'll take very good care of her," I said.

The young woman didn't look at me. The bottom of the large overcoat she was wearing dragged along the driveway as we walked to the car. I thought it was getting dirty and I tried to take her arm, but she pulled away and mumbled something like "is good, is good." The winter chill still hung in the air, so perhaps she was wearing this man's coat for warmth. When I opened the backseat door for her and started to help her in, she pulled away and said, "No, no, fine," without looking at me. I wondered if she didn't want me to see her face.

As I was about to start the motor, I saw that the stout lady was still standing in her doorway, looking at us. I waved politely and turned to ask the young woman where she wanted to go.

"New York," she said.

"Yes," I answered, "your mother—or whoever that nice lady is—told me that. But where in New York?"

"One . . . five . . . three . . . East Fifty-three Street," she answered.

"One fifty-three East Fifty-third?" I asked, to make sure I understood.

"That's why I just say it," she said.

"Fine," I said, and drove off.

While we were on the Saw Mill River Parkway, well on our way to New York, I thought I'd try a little conversation, just to be friendly.

"By the way, my name is Max Baer." But there was no answer.

"Excuse me," I said, "but what do you want me to call you? I was never given your name."

"Katarina Nováková," she said.

"Wow! Well, I might be able to handle that," I said, trying to lighten the atmosphere.

"You don't have to handle. You just say it."

"No, I mean—would you mind if I just called you Miss or Ma'am?"

"You mean you want to be more friendlier?"

"Well, yes . . . but not if it bothers you."

"Call me Katka," she said.

"Katka?"

"What?"

"No, I mean—you really want me to call you Katka?"

"That's why I say it."

"Of course! Thank you."

She must have seen my puzzlement in the rearview mirror.

"Is short for Katarina," she said, "which is maybe too complicated for you. I don't mean to insult—is just that nicknames are more friendlier, yes?"

"Absolutely," I said. "Thank you."

"And yours?" she asked.

"My name is Max, but . . . a few people call me Maxie, if you should ever want to use my nickname."

"For sure, Maxie."

This is an interesting woman, I thought to myself. And smarter than I expected. I wonder why I didn't think she was smart . . . just because of that frozen grin on her face, which still hasn't changed even when she talks pleasantly?

The East River looked beautiful in the late afternoon sunlight. We didn't talk very much for most of the trip, but when we passed the UN building I saw her gazing at it with bright eyes.

"You know Czech Republic?" she asked.

"Of course," I said.

"Is where I'm from," she said.

"Oh. Was it Czech you were speaking with your mother?"

"Eva's not my mother—she was my father's mistress. I never saw my mother, but Eva takes care of me like I'm her baby."

"And does your father live with you?" I asked.

"My father is dead five months."

"I'm sorry."

"He goes to Brooklyn to visit Russian film director friend—my father was beautiful designer for movie posters, Czech films, foreign films, all kinds—and some Russian punks shoot him when he doesn't give up his wallet."

"I'm sorry, Katka."

"Me too," she said.

Silence for a minute, but I didn't want to leave things on that sad note.

"May I ask if that's your father's coat you're wearing?"

"Yes. You think is too big for me?"

"Well, it's just that—"

She started to laugh. "Of course is too big for me. But I like to wear it—not always, just sometimes—when I'm little nervous. It makes me feel like my Papa is still holding me. You think I'm silly woman?"

"No, I don't think so," I said.

We approached East Fifty-third Street.

"We're almost there, Katka."

"Is two more blocks, on left side."

When we reached 153 I saw a sign in bold letters that read: Walton Gallery.

"Is this where you want to go? The gallery?"

"Yes. Go into parking," she said.

As we entered the dark underground parking floor that was next door to the gallery, the parking attendant seemed to know the Oldsmobile, and when he saw Katka he immediately waved and opened her door. They spoke together for a few seconds in what must have been Czech. Then she took off her father's coat and placed it gently on the backseat.

Without her father's coat, I was surprised at what a beautiful figure she had. She was wearing a flowing white skirt and a white blouse that was trimmed with pink around the collar. When she straightened her beret, I could see how pretty her bright red hair was that crept down her forehead.

"You want to come in, Maxie?" she asked. "They're going to hang me."

"You don't mean 'hang you,' Katka," I said with a smile, assuming that her English wasn't quite what she intended.

"Yes, for sure. They promised. Come, you don't have to fix your tie—you look nice. You are handsome man, Maxie."

I followed her up a small staircase and through a metal door and we walked into the Walton Gallery. A distinguished-looking gentleman came up quickly. He and Katka kissed each other on both cheeks and spoke in Czech. Then she yanked my sleeve to come closer.

"Karal Straka, this is my friendly Mister Max Baer."

We shook hands. "So pleased to meet you, Mr. Baer. And now, Katka—are you ready to see your room?"

"Yes, please," she said.

Mr. Straka led us to a room at the end of the hall.

"I'll leave you to be with your work, Katka, and I'll keep other people out of the room for as long as you wish. I hope you like the way we hung your two beauties."

I realized, of course, that she was obviously a painter. She was telling the truth about being hung. The joke was on me.

"Just open the door and wave to me when you're done," Mr. Straka said. When we were inside the room he closed the door.

I followed Katka, expecting to see some pleasant country scenes, but the two enormous paintings that hung in front of me took my breath away.

On the left was a painting of a completely naked man lying on a couch, apparently asleep. He was middle-aged, with short, dark hair, almost handsome but not quite. The shadows on his naked body emphasized his small feet, his long penis, his underarm hair, and the slight bags under his eyes.

To the right was a painting of a completely naked woman.

She was lying sensuously on a similar couch, facing the man. She had dark brown eyes and was thin, but with enormous breasts. One of her eyes was wide open, looking at the naked man. Both of the paintings had nondescript backgrounds of a soft peach color.

I kept staring at the paintings and after several seconds tears came to my eyes.

"So? What you think?" Katka asked.

I tried to speak, but couldn't get any words out at first.

"Not what I expected," I finally said.

"Why you are crying? Please tell me."

"I went to art school years ago. I wanted to paint. It was the only thing I wanted to do in my life but I wasn't really very good, even though I tried so hard."

"Okay, now I change subjects. You like big breasts?"

"What do you mean?"

"This is not difficult question. When you are with women, you like big breasts—like this woman in my painting—or you like small breasts?" she asked.

"To tell you the truth, Katka . . . I've always been a little afraid of women with large breasts."

"Afraid they are going to bite you?" she asked.

"No, I wasn't afraid of that. But I always felt more comfortable with women who had small breasts."

"You mean, like with little woman, like me?" she asked with a lascivious look in her eyes.

I started laughing and wiped the leftover tears from my eyes. "Well, I haven't seen your breasts."

"Okay, maybe later," she said. "Right now, I'm hungry. Oh! One more question. Are you married?"

"Not any more," I said.

"Okay, good. I'm still hungry."

Katka opened the door and waved. Mr. Straka came walking to her with a bounce in his step.

"Did we do all right, Katka?" he asked.

She gave him a kiss on both cheeks again. "Fantastique!" she said. "Now we go eat."

We walked out the front door of the gallery and stepped onto the busy sidewalk.

"You want to go to dinner?" Katka asked.

"With you?"

"No, with the garbage collector. Who you think I'm asking?"

"Well, don't get so huffy, Miss Czechoslovakia Nova Scotia. I'm your driver and I wasn't sure if you wanted to do some shopping, or do something else while I went somewhere to eat."

"Hmm. Okay, forget logical. Praga is right around corner. Very good restaurant. You like Czech food?"

"I've never had it."

"Good. Take my arm and I don't push you away this time, and we go to Praga."

"Is that short for Prague?"

"Yes, is a nickname," she said as she winked at me. "Come, we walk all the way to Prague."

We were greeted royally when we entered Praga, which was made to look like an old-world Czech restaurant, I assumed, with its soft yellowish lights and shiny mahogany walls. A man who must have been the owner rushed up when he saw Katka and lifted her off the floor. When he set her down they kissed each other on both cheeks.

"Max—this is owner of my stomach and also this restaurant, Mister Ivo Malek. Ivo—here is my good friend Mister Max Baer, who never in his life has eaten Czech food."

Mr. Malek shook my hand vigorously and then showed us to a somewhat private booth. He signaled to a waiter, who actually ran to Katka. They jabbered away in Czech and laughed about something Katka said while they were looking at me. When she introduced me to Ivan he, too, shook my hand vigorously.

"You like lager beer?" Katka asked.

"Oh, yes," I said.

"Two Krušovice, Ivan."

"Of course." he answered, and, like Mr. Straka in the gallery, he skipped away.

Katka looked at me with quizzical eyes.

"How come you don't ask?"

"Ask what, Katka?"

"About my stupid grin."

"It's not my business."

"You have ever heard of the Bell's palsy?"

"Yes."

"I got it frozen onto my face for six months. But my dentist says this stupid grin will go away very soon and I will be beautiful again. What you think?"

"After seeing you without your father's coat on . . . and after seeing your paintings . . . I would say that you are already beautiful."

"Ahh! Now my driver is also diplomat."

"No, you're wrong. I meant what I said."

She studied me for a few seconds without speaking. When our beer arrived she raised her glass and said: "Skol!"

Ivan, our friendly waiter, looked at me while I took my first sip of Krošovice. After a big swallow I looked up at him.

"Delicious!"

"Thank you, sir," he said. "And now for dinner—"

"Oh, you pick for us, Ivan," Katka said. "Surprise us." Ivan smiled and walked away quickly.

"What a brave choice, Katka."

"I am brave woman," she answered.

Ivan brought an assortment of food on a large wooden tray and placed it in the center of our table. When Katka saw how wide my eyes grew, she began to laugh.

"What you bring us today, Ivan?" Katka asked.

"Roast duck with red cabbage and dumplings . . . beef with some dill sauce . . . and a little roast pork with fruit dumplings. Just a little bit of each," Ivan said with a happy grin. "Please enjoy. I'll bring you more beer right away. Thank you."

Katka watched me take my first bite. "These fruit dumplings are almost heaven," I said.

"They are not so good in heaven. This is just normal Czech cooking."

Two hours later I drove this unusual woman back to her home.

"You should have let me pay for dinner, Katka. I ate three times more than you."

"You don't pay first time. Was my treat. Are you all right for driving?"

"Beer doesn't affect me like wine or whiskey. I'm fine."

"Good. May we have a little music, Maxie?"

"What kind?"

"Good music," she answered.

I put the radio on one of the classical stations and heard the middle of the piece by Dvořák called "Songs My Mother Taught Me." I loved it because it was so peaceful and always made me feel that there was really nothing to worry about.

"Oh, good," Katka said when she heard the music, and then drifted off to sleep.

When we arrived at her home, I helped my tiny old-world client to the door. Eva, the stout lady, opened it before Katka could put her key in.

"Oh, Eva," Katka said as she fell into the stout lady's arms and kissed her. "We had such wonderful time. No more Mister Baer for this beautiful man—just Maxie now. He liked my paintings, Eva—so much that he cried. Can you believe? So you must be very nice to him."

Eva smiled and shook my hand. "You took good care of my girl. Thank you, Mister Max."

"I want to show him my studio," Katka said.

"Of course you do," Eva answered. "But you're sleepy now, my little flower, and maybe a little tipsy, so how about tomorrow?"

"Will you come tomorrow, Maxie? Please?" Katka implored.

"I'm free after four in the afternoon. Will that be all right?"

"Wonderful," she said. "I see you tomorrow."

Katka leaned over and kissed me on both cheeks, as she did to her Czech friends, but her lips lingered on my cheeks a little longer than on theirs.

"I am very happy, Mister Maxie. I hope you have good dreams," she said as Eva helped her into the house.

Adorable woman, I thought to myself as I was driving home. I suppose she puts on such a strong front to cover how vulnerable she must feel because of her frozen grin. You'd better be careful with her, Mister Maxie.

The next morning I had a nine thirty pickup at LaGuardia Airport. After I took my client to his home in Manhattan,

I drove to Westport to pick up an elderly couple for a two o'clock drop-off at JFK Airport. While I was there I had an omelet and a cup of coffee, freshened up a little in the men's room, and then drove to Katka's home.

As I pulled up to the farmhouse Eva was just coming out of the front door. "She's in her studio, Mister Max . . . the little barn across the field. You want something to eat?"

"No, I just had lunch. Thank you, Eva."

"Good," she said. "I have to go to Greenwich now to waste my time with a doctor. When I come back I don't disturb you unless you get hungry. Then you just holler 'EVA' and I come running," she said as she gave me a hug.

It's strange how put off I was when I met Eva—I suppose because I was slightly frightened by her size and how imposing she was—and now I adored her for the loving way she took care of Katka, and for her warm acceptance of me.

I walked across the small field toward the barn. No sheep or cows, but a great many birds and butterflies flying in and out of trees and bushes. They all seemed very much at home. When I reached the barn I saw that the Dutch door was already open. I called out "Yoo-hoo" as I peeked in.

"Yoo-hoo," I heard Katka calling back rather softly.

When I walked into the dimly lit barn I saw Katka lying on a comfortable-looking couch, in much the same pose as the naked lady in her painting, except that Katka wasn't naked; she was wearing a very loose-fitting paint-splattered smock.

"Where's the naked man on your other couch?" I asked.

"Come in and maybe we find out," she said in a somber tone that didn't seem like her. I walked closer and saw resting on a large easel a half-finished self-portrait of Katka. She was wearing a yellow beret.

"Is everything all right, Katka?"

"I'm good *now* and happy to see you, *except*—I don't look good in yellow. I never look good in yellow, so why in hell do I paint myself in yellow beret? Okay, I know why . . . so that you take your eyes away from my stupid grin, which doctor promises will go away any week or month or year now."

"I didn't see the frozen grin in your painting."

"Of course! With paint is very easy to make it go away. Never mind. Come sit by me and take off your jacket."

I took off my jacket and sat next to her.

"Take off your tie, too—you're not driving cars and I'm not your client now. So tell me—how you are, Mister Maxie?"

"I'm very good. I worked all morning and now I can rest."

"Good," she said. "I want to ask a question."

"Sure."

"When was last time you had test for sex diseases?"

It took me a few moments to recover, but of course the sudden frankness of her question was just like her.

"Six months, just before my divorce."

"And?"

"And everything was fine."

"Good! Any sex since six months?"

"I haven't thought about sex since then," I said.

"Hmm. Is about time, you don't think?"

"Are you making a real suggestion, Katka, or are you just playing with me?"

"I am making real suggestion *because* I want to play with you," she said very seriously. It was a little difficult for me not to laugh.

"What about babies, Katka?"

"You want babies??" she asked.

"No, I mean—do you have something to prevent babies? I don't travel with condoms."

"I have IDU in me," she said.

"You mean you have an IUD in you."

"I just say so," Katka answered. "Relax about babies. Maybe we have some later. Oh, look here—I find some vodka right next to me. Some accident, huh? You want little sip? It gives me courage."

"All right, just a little sip."

"Good! Take off your pants and I give you little sip."

Katka saw me holding back a laugh as I took off my pants. "Good for you," she said. "Is good to laugh. Maybe I give up painting and just make people laugh. What you think?"

"Don't give up painting, Katka."

"Okay, take off your underwear and is a deal."

I took off my boxer shorts.

"Oh my! You have got something there. I think I could use that," she said.

As she took off her painter's smock and exposed her naked body, she suddenly became nervous. After all that talk I realized that she was shy. She looked away from me and back again, almost giggled twice, and then became very serious. My guess is that she was self-conscious about her frozen grin and was afraid she wouldn't be able to live up to the wisecracking front she'd been putting on. Well, I was nervous too. I hadn't been with a woman for a long time and I wasn't sure if I was doing the right thing by encouraging Katka's sexual behavior. And yet . . . I was very attracted to her.

I sat down next to her, took her face into my hands, and gently kissed her. She stiffened at first, but after a minute or two I could taste the salt from her tears.

Later that evening, when I was about to leave, Katka put her arms around my chest and hugged me.

"Will I see you ever again, Mister Maxie?"

"If you make me laugh again."

"I'm going to find good jokes," she said.

"Then I'll see you whenever you wish."

"And you won't mind kissing my stupid grin?" she asked.

"I'll be kissing you, Katka . . . not your frozen grin."

". . . Can I see you tomorrow?" she asked like a child.

"If you want, but I'll be so tired from driving until ten

o'clock at night . . . would you mind if it was the next day?"

"Okay, deal! Wednesday!" she said and hugged me again as hard as she could, which wasn't really that hard.

That night I dreamed that I was swimming underwater with Katka, who was a mermaid. Her beautiful face didn't have the frozen grin but there were scales all over her little body and long tail. I could pick off a scale and see it float away, but each time I did another scale would pop up. I kept picking and picking while I held my breath, but I was running out of air. I signaled to Katka that I had to leave her and swim up in order to breathe. She stared at me as I swam away.

I finished late on Wednesday afternoon, took a hot shower, changed into fresh clothes, and went to see Katka.

I think Eva must have been expecting me. When I pulled into the driveway she came out hurriedly, like a traffic cop, and waved me on toward the studio. I parked my car and as soon as I walked through the open Dutch doors Katka ran up to me with a worried look and flushed face. She was wearing what looked like a doctor's lab coat.

"Quick," she said in a panic. "You know what ko-lacky is?"

"No. Is it serious, Katka?"

"I don't think so—it's just pastry Eva made for us," and she burst out laughing. "Was that good joke?"

I was angry for only a moment and then pretended to spank her for scaring me.

"So, you *do* like me. Good! Come sit and we have some kolacky."

"But why are you wearing a doctor's lab coat?"

"Is not for real doctors. I throw away my old smock because it has paint all over and I don't want you to smell paint when you come near to me. Eat some cake. Eva made special for us."

I took a bite of kolacky. It tasted like a very subtly spiced cheesecake with some other ingredients that I couldn't identify. "Mmmm, this is delicious. What did she put in here?"

"Cream cheese, honey, nutmeg . . . who knows? You want big piece?"

"Not yet."

"You want me?" she asked with a twinkle in her eyes. "I taste good too."

I nodded yes.

She hugged me and pulled me onto the soft couch. We made love again but it was different this time. She didn't cry while we were making love, she laughed. I couldn't figure her out.

Afterwards, Katka had a nice supper waiting for us that she heated up on her studio hotplate. Eva had cooked a veal, beef, and pork meatloaf and we drank a Belgian beer I had never heard of.

While we ate we talked about portrait painting, which I thought I knew a little about, but Katka had an almost encyclopedic knowledge of European painters, going back as far as the Renaissance.

"Who is your favorite, Maxie?"

"I love so many painters," I said as I stuffed my mouth with more of Eva's meatloaf. "But my two favorites are Manet and Renoir."

"Those guys were blessed," she said.

"Do you have a favorite, Katka?"

"*You* are my favorite, silly boy."

"Painters!" I said.

"Oooh . . . Kandinsky, Goya, Velázquez, Mary Cassatt, Rubens . . . too many favorites," she said.

It was getting late. I told her that I had to get up early the next morning to go to Boston for three days on business. Then the tears began to flow.

"Now don't cry, please. I'll be back before you can say Jack Robinson, Katka."

I knew she wouldn't have a clue what that meant, and probably wouldn't be able to say it even if she did. I just wanted to say something silly to comfort her.

"If I say it, you come back?"

"Of course."

"Jack Rabbit has son Katka . . . that's what you say?"

". . . Yes, that's what I said. Well—here I am!"

"H'm! You trick me." She gave me a big smile and we kissed good night.

When we reached Boston, my clients went to a seminar on holistic medicine at the Marriott Copley Place hotel. The husband told me to pick them up in three hours. I put their Cadillac into a nearby parking garage, and, since it was a fairly warm afternoon, I took a walk along Huntington Avenue. When I passed the Museum of Fine Arts I saw a gigantic red sign at the top of the stairs that read: RENOIR EXHIBITION. I went in.

Walking through each room was like visiting dear friends whom I hadn't seen in many years. When I came to Renoir's famous *Dance at Bougival* I was stunned. I stared at it like an imbecile. The tall man in the painting—who wore a huge straw hat that covered most of his face except for his nose and beard—was dancing with Katka . . . and she was wearing the same white dress and blouse that she wore the first time I saw her . . . and the same red hat . . . and she had the same adorable tiny lips and baby fingers.

I began to sweat. The tall man in the straw hat was making his amorous intentions only too obvious. He was holding Katka so tightly that I became jealous. I moved closer so that she could hear me.

"Katka," I said softly. "Don't listen to this tall asshole.

His beard would scratch your face to pieces if he ever kissed you the way I kiss you." I moved closer and whispered, "I love you, Katka."

As I raised my hand to touch her beautiful face, a guard rushed up and shouted: "SIR—YOU CAN'T TOUCH HER! Stay behind the white line. Please!" he said in a threatening voice.

"But she's *my* girl. The tall jerk with the straw hat is . . . is . . ." and I suddenly realized where I was.

"I'm sorry," I said as I backed away. "I wasn't going to harm her, I promise. I had a bad shock today, that's all. I'm fine now. Please forgive me."

The guard looked at me as if he wasn't quite sure what to do: Was I a poor fellow who didn't feel well . . . or was I some nut who should be locked up?

"You'd better get out of here and get some fresh air," he said almost kindly.

"I will," I said. "You're right . . . I just need a little air."

Driving back to Greenwich with my clients, I was grateful they hardly spoke to me during the whole trip; too busy talking with each other about the lecture they heard and all the vegetarians they met.

As I was driving, the only thing that filled my brain was: Why did I reach out to touch Katka in the museum? . . . not a painting that looked like her, but actually Katka? And why did I get jealous of that tall schmuck in the straw hat who was too chicken to show his face and yet not at all afraid to show off the sexy way he was holding . . . oh my God . . . I'm borderline psychotic. Keep your eyes on the road or you're going to have an accident.

It was seven thirty and almost dark when I reached Katka's house. As I walked closer to the open Dutch doors my heart began pounding hard. Why? Of course I'm anxious to see her again . . . but nervous?

I heard one of Haydn's trios floating out softly from her studio. When I saw that Katka was asleep on the couch I tiptoed in and was about to surprise her when she suddenly spoke, with her eyes still closed.

"What makes you think I sleep when I wait for you?" she said.

"Because I could hear you snoring all the way out in the driveway," I answered.

She opened her eyes. "I don't snore! And I make better jokes than you make. Did you miss me in Boston?"

"I saw you in Boston."

"You didn't see me. I was here."

"I did see you. You were right in front of me, dancing with some tall man in a straw hat. I almost got arrested when I tried to touch you."

"H'm. Not such funny joke, but very romantic," she said as she held out her arms to me.

While we made love on her couch, I was the one who

wept this time. For a few moments I didn't even know where I was . . . I just knew that I loved her.

On a sunny July day three months later, we were married by a judge in the small field next to Katka's studio. Her frozen grin was almost gone and during the ceremony she couldn't stop smiling. Her father's overcoat and Eva were our only guests.